TRANSFORMATIONS

AN OXFORD FLASH FICTION PRIZE
ANTHOLOGY

F J MORRIS

First published by Oxford Flash Fiction Prize CIC in 2024.

Cover design by Dot Little at the Bodleian Library.

ISBN-13: 9781739209759

CONTENTS

INTRODUCTION

2024 marks a hundred years since the death of one of the greatest flash fiction writers of all time, Franz Kafka, who arguably mastered the form before it had even come into being. In partnership with the Bodleian Libraries' *Kafka: Making of an Icon* exhibition at the University of Oxford, the 2024 Oxford Flash Fiction prize marks this centenary and celebrates Kafka's astonishing literary achievements and vibrant creativity. In honour of the longest completed work of fiction we have from Kafka's pen – 'The Metamorphosis' – the stories collected in this volume explore the theme of transformations.

None of Kafka's three posthumously published novels was ever finished, but his shorter works of fiction – some barely a few lines long – are gems whose sparkle never dulls. The devil really is in the detail. In an untitled piece composed in 1920 that is less than a page long, Kafka tells the story of a tireless philosopher obsessed with a spinning top: 'He believed', Kafka writes, 'that the knowledge of any little thing, including a spinning top, for instance, sufficed to know everything. [...] If the smallest detail was really known, then everything was known, so he only concerned himself with the spinning top.' But keeping a spinning top spinning is a fleeting endeavour, and the philosopher becomes breathless from chasing after it. Holding it in his hands, having finally caught it, he's left reeling, Kafka notes, 'like a spinning top lashed by a clumsy whip.' Composing flash fiction, I can only imagine, is a lot like keeping a top spinning. Reading this year's entries also left me reeling. Unlike the philosopher in Kafka's story, however, I didn't feel queasy and alarmed as he does when he realises that he's interrupted children at play by snatching away their toy. Rather, I felt exhilarated and privileged to have the chance to marvel at these whirling wonderful creations.

As one of the researchers on the "Kafka's Transformative Communities" project, funded by the Arts and Humanities Research Council, I was thrilled to be asked to serve as one of the judges for the 2024 prize. I owe a profound debt of gratitude to Freya Morris, first and foremost, for her invitation and her guidance; to my fellow judges, Deesha Philyaw and Avi Ben-Zeev, for their sensitive insights and good humour; to the Bodleian's public engagement team for making the partnership happen; to the readers who compiled such a fantastic shortlist; and to all the writers whose work appears in the following pages for the hours of wonder their words inspired. It was a truly transformative experience for me and my fellow judges to read what follows.

Dr Ian Ellison, October 2024

PART I

'A CAGE WENT IN SEARCH OF A BIRD.'

FRANZ KAFKA, THE THIRD OCTAVO NOTEBOOK, TRANSLATED BY ERNST KAISER AND EITHNE WILKINS

Today, I woke up with the sun shining through my eyelids, tickling my eyeballs and flicking the switch to open them up. My eyes felt blurry as I tried to open them. They wouldn't open. I rubbed them, walked to the bathroom to bathe them with warm water. Still they wouldn't open. What should I do? Who should I call? I couldn't find my mobile. I checked my pockets but there was nothing but receipts, ripped up evidence of past frivolous purchases – things collected to try and add some value to my life. What is my purpose now? Do I need value or is this a lie told to us when we are young? Now I grow old or I grow younger? Shrinking backwards through the years like Benjamin Button. Like Brad Pitt. Oh to be Brad Pitt!

An 'exquisite corpse' micro-fiction from Bodleian Libraries' writing workshops

1

WHEN THE STORK BROUGHT ELIZA A ROCK INSTEAD OF A BABY

BY KATJA SASS

Wednesday

When the maid opened the curtains a shard of light, the first Eliza had seen in five months, landed on the bright white top-feathers, then the slender, blood-red beak, of a stork sitting by her feet. Between her legs was the rock.

The rock was misshapen, grey, marbled by shades of dark purple, with one knotted white ribbon by its side, maybe the linen it had been carried in. The rock caught some of the light and shone a little. Eliza felt a light inside her too, something like love, what little she had been told of it.

Her mother's voice seeped in from outside the room like a foul smell: *No more babies.*

The stork looked sad, as though it hadn't known it was bringing her a rock, not a baby.

Thursday

Eliza spent the day in her bed, in pain, in confusion.

The stork lay close but did not touch her. It hid the rock

under its wing, the darkening grey of the stone barely distinguishable from the black feathers on the wing's tips.

Eliza heard her mother's voice outside the room, *We can't let her touch it.*

Friday

The stork was watching her when she woke. It had grown, and now gazed down at her, its eyes large and brown, like a human's.

Saturday

Eliza had been awake all night but now, as the sun rose, she found herself able to stretch her hand as far as the rock and touch it for the first time.

As the stork slept, Eliza pulled the rock to her. It was smooth against her fingers, but heavy. It didn't move easily.

She put it against her swollen breast, but it wouldn't suckle. It was cold against her skin. She took the dark shawl from her shoulders and wrapped it around the rock.

Outside the bedroom, Eliza heard her mother's voice, *It's disgusting, it's rotten.*

Eliza turned to her side and curled her body around the rock, drifting back to sleep.

Sunday

Eliza was told she was not quite well enough to go to church with the family in the morning. *We cannot let this into God's house*, the mother explained to the doctor.

In the late afternoon gloom, somebody entered the room and placed their hands under the rock. Eliza, though drowsy, felt the weight of the bed shift slightly.

The stork raised itself to full height and held out its wings.

Eliza heard her mother whisper, *We have to take it away from her*. But when the stork didn't move, she began to step backwards and left the room.

The stork made itself smaller again then came and rested its head against Eliza's leg. The window, now open a little, brought a breeze that moved its feathers lightly against her skin, the softness surprising her.

Monday

It has no soul, and you have driven Eliza mad by letting her keep it.

The thin woman was in the doorway, addressing the stork. The bird stood at full height, obscuring the figure of her mother.

It looked over at the bed where Eliza lay watching, still clutching the rock to her, but it didn't say anything. Instead, it stood back, craned its long, graceful neck, and nudged the door shut with its beak.

That night, after she had closed the curtains, Eliza walked to the sleeping stork and drew its feathers through her fingers. She lay next to the bird until morning.

Tuesday

They took the rock out with them in a pram. Eliza wanted to feel the air on her skin.

A passer-by held a delicate handkerchief over her face and moved out onto the road so as not to walk by them. The stork spread out its vast wings, placing them all in shadow, until the woman rushed away.

Eliza stepped under the stork's outstretched wing. *I love*

you, she said quietly. *Thank you.* She liked the bird's warmth, its breath, the way its heart quickened when she touched it.

Then, feeling somehow neglectful, she brushed the rock lightly with her hand and said *I love you, too.*

That night Eliza slept next to the stork again. She left the rock in a basket, where it was slowly turning the straw black.

Wednesday

Eliza opened the curtains and drew her cloak around her.

On the floor beside her, the stork placed the bare rock onto white linen before gently pulling each corner together with its beak. It lifted the rock slowly, tired and aged.

They walked through the town at dawn until they arrived at the woods near the lake. Eliza got down on her knees and placed the rock on the ground. She and the stalk moved the soil to surround and eventually cover it. Eliza pressed a makeshift cross from twigs into the small mound.

Eliza and the stork stood together by the rock's grave until it went dark. As they walked back through the town, she noticed a trail of black and white feathers, the bird becoming naked so that they could always follow the path back to their rock.

That night, Eliza was woken by her mother's voice again.

It's over, the stork whispered back.

Eliza recognised the voice, recalled her husband's large, brown eyes.

He switched off the light and came back to bed. She felt his tears on her neck as he curled up around her.

It wasn't his fault, she thought, that he had given her a rock instead of a baby.

When the stork brought Eliza a rock instead of a baby by Katja Sass © 2024

Katja Sass teaches philosophy and religion at a UK secondary school, subjects that often find their way into the pieces somehow. Her stories can be found at Lost Futures, Ekphrastic Review, Janus Literary and Paragraph Planet, and have won prizes at Reflex Fiction and Writers' Playground. She can be found on X as @catchersass.

2

MORE SKY THAN ANYWHERE

THIRD PLACE PRIZE WINNER

BY CHRIS COTTOM

By the morning, the storm has blown itself out but left the village with no electricity. We wrap up and stroll down the hill to the ramshackle barn where, in faded black paint, a sign proclaims 'Veg in Shed'. I point out the cluster of nests under the eaves and you tell me to expect the swallows back in April, that they'll fly six thousand miles from Africa, but not in a straight line.

On an old door laid across some crates are a bunch of carrots with the green bits tied in red baling twine, a rubble of muddy potatoes, and an untrimmed Savoy cabbage on which a brace of slugs are copulating. There's a battered Quality Street tin for the money and an enamelled set of scales pocked with scabs of rust, with a platform for the weights, but no actual weights.

Back in the cottage, we peel and chop and you tell me about teaching sewing skills at an orphanage in Tamil Nadu, a day's drive from Chennai; your elder twin sisters, both married with kids; your plans for a working holiday in Australia. I tell you it's been a lifesaver, coming up here every weekend, building a log store, going to hotpot suppers in the village hall. I tell you what they say here, that Suffolk has more sky than anywhere.

We put the pan on the woodburning stove and head out again, along the back lane they call the Road to Nowhere, until it becomes a track, then narrows to a path. When this peters out, we climb a stile to skirt a ploughed field up to the wood, where it's alternately mud-slippy or loamy with leaf mould. You chatter about grumpy goblins, elves dancing with nymphs, dairymaids cavorting with their swains beneath the gnarly oaks. Avoiding snares of barbed briars, we emerge at the far side where, across the sodden fields towards Lavenham, black clouds are menacing the pewter sky.

By the time we get back to the track, it's a stream. Before we reach the tiny village green, our boots are squelchy sponges. Ditching our sopping clothes in the kitchen, we try to rub one another warm under a tepid shower before snuggling in front of the stove, your soft ginger hair turbaned in a towel.

It's dark by half-past four and we light my emergency candles. When you say it's like a church and perhaps we should pray, I'm not sure you're joking. We squint at last week's *Observer* before feasting on our hearty soup, relishing its heat and congratulating ourselves on being so resourceful. After thrashing me twice at Scrabble, you place the sofa cushions neatly in front of the hearth and unbutton your dress.

In the morning, the electricity is back on and we walk in the other direction, across the empty fields and along through the meadows to Chelsworth. We stand on the bridge, watching the swollen river surging through, and you explain that swallows stop over in reed beds to sleep while they're migrating, up to a million in the same place, like an enormous bird motel.

Later, you're quiet after I lock up and we head south through Halstead and Braintree. Before we reach the motorway, you've fallen asleep. As we stop-start through the London traffic, you jerk awake and navigate me to Forest Gate, where you ask me to drop you at the corner, rather than drive down your road. When I ask you about next weekend, you say you'll let me know, that things are a bit complicated. You hurry into the dark, your bag over your shoulder, and I wonder why swallows don't travel in a straight line. As I drive away, I remember you saying that half of them return to the same nest.

Chris Cottom lives near Macclesfield, UK. He's packed Christmas hampers in a Harrods basement, sold airtime for Radio Luxembourg, and served a twelve-year stretch as an insurance copywriter. He liked the writing job best.

@chris_cottom1

chriscottom.wixsite.com/chriscottom

3

CORVIDS

BY GC PERRY

We're ten days into this and Joe has become increasingly distant. He spends hours in his study. We meet at mealtimes but conversation is stilted. He seems stunned: unable to take in this bizarre turn of events. On the rare occasions his eyes meet mine, there is a something there I don't recognise. An absence? An emptiness?

,

The warmer weather has arrived and this has brought Joe from his study more frequently. We sit in the backyard together: I, reading or working on the laptop, Joe staring vacantly at the floor, or the sky, or making notes in an exercise book he's taken to carrying around with him. When I ask him what he's writing, he just tells me that he's recording: 'Thoughts. Nothing really.' He will not be drawn, and I don't want to upset him and force him back to his study. With the warmth of the spring sun, and Joe's proximity, I feel a kind of peace. But it feels neither stable nor permanent.

,

Two nights ago, Joe took his pillows and a blanket and now he sleeps in his study. He tells me he is worried that his boyhood asthma puts him at risk. He feels vulnerable. I miss his presence in the bed.

,

Today, in the backyard, Joe turns to me fiercely: 'Fucking magpies!' There are four or five of them hopping in the sycamore that overhangs our property. The clatter of the branches and their harsh, rasping chatter seem maddening to him. He retreats to his study. I watch the birds: the purple-green shimmer amidst the black. I have never before noticed their long pluming tail feathers.

,

Joe is more withdrawn than ever. He is taking his meals in his study now. I listen at his door. Sometimes I hear a frantic, insect twitching and tapping. Other times, it is silent. It's cloudy today and there's a chill to the wind. I work in the living room on my laptop. I have the TV on with the sound turned down. ITV4: The Sweeney, Kojak, Quincey.

,

Joe emerges from his study. He has made some kind of contraption, I later discover, out of two wicker wastepaper baskets and a larger basket we use to keep firewood in. There is something beautiful about it. 'The magpies,' is all he will say. I watch as he takes it to the backyard and places it next to a potted hydrangea. It is a bird trap which he baits with a small handful of seeds. I say nothing but for the first time I start to feel afraid.

,

The trap has worked. I come down for breakfast to see Joe standing over the rattling wicker trap, flickers of black and white intermittently visible as the bird struggles against its prison. 'Joe!' I plead. It's no use. He slips his hand into the trap and the magpie's clattering protests fill the air. I cannot watch. I take my toast and return to bed.

,

Days have passed and Joe and I remain remote. I think he may have taken more birds. He scares me. I feel trapped. There seems no end to this.

,

I am walking the deserted streets of South London in the midnight drizzle. It is quiet except for the occasional strains of music and young voices from a few still-lit windows. A gust of wind makes an orange puddle glitter in the street-lighted night. I did not see Joe today.

,

We're six weeks in now. Joe comes to me in the night. His body is half-lit by the dull glow of the landing light. He is naked. His skin looks yellow and is taut across jutting bones and tight, knotty muscles. I see his semi-erect penis bobbing between his legs. On his head he wears a headdress like a Native American chief. He leans over me and I feel the feathers brush against my skin. A glint of pearlescent green, a glimmer of metallic purple. I see Joe's hand reaching and I feel him touch my hipbone. I open myself to him. None of this makes any sense to me. I do it anyway.

4

NORTHBOUND

FINALIST

BY AMANDA O'CALLAGHAN

He knows it's close, though he can barely see the road, rain streaming across the windscreen. Early autumn. Grey as winter, already. William had forgotten how it could be. There's the metal sign, up on the hill, unchanged. Any moment, now. He shakes his head, feels the familiar churn in his gut. There's the entrance. He turns in without warning. A van behind him whooshes past, a muffled blare of horn in its wake. It's been years. Decades. The sudden stilling of the motorway's roar. William had forgotten that, too. The way it eased him, somehow.

The driveway's been widened, the hedges trimmed back. The big oak at the front is gone. The place looks newer, fresher. William manoeuvres into his old spot, squints through the rain at the broad, square windows, starry points of light over the tables, a sense of movement behind the foggy glass. Above the main door, a square of bright cursive still blinks its neon-orange *Welcome.*

William scratches his head, trying to steady his thoughts, wishes he still smoked to calm his fretful hands. He glances at the box on the passenger seat, the overnight bag in the footwell. The rain's beginning to slow. A thin man hurries from his car, flicking raindrops from his jacket sleeves, smoothing back his dampened hair. He looks like I did thirty years ago, William thinks, turning off the engine.

'Surprised you didn't try for the promotion,' his colleague had said, leaning on William's desk. 'You're much better qualified. More money.' William had toyed with his fountain pen, picked at the scales of paper clips clinging to a magnetised pyramid. 'Maybe next year,' he said, feeling panic slither in the hollowed out spaces within him, knowing he couldn't stand it much longer. How the yearning he had for other places, far from here, coursed through him like an addiction, like poison. Another life, waiting somewhere. Not screeching to a halt, hard against the brewery wall, like his father. Or crumbling to the factory floor like his grandfather. Not draping his own misery in two pink-skinned weeks on the coast. A whole life, somewhere south of here. But Roslyn. She couldn't bear the thought of leaving England. She loved her rose garden, her sisters, the narrow streets of her childhood.

'I can't do it,' she told him. 'I won't do it.'

William let his dreams go, but headaches seared through him, his bones ached when he walked. His doctor could find nothing wrong, suggested a fortnight in the sun.

Promotion washed towards him like a tide. He bought a new car, renovated the kitchen. His neighbour taught him to fish, amazed at William's patient skill until one day, clubbing a struggling salmon, William screamed until the woods echoed. They'd travelled home in silence, never mentioning it again.

After work, William began to watch for the lights, the broad shoulders of the services building jutting from the hillside. A car or two would peel off the motorway ahead of him, rise through the curved hedges. One evening, William followed. A quick break, he told himself. Clear his head. Soon, he was stopping every night. There was no explaining it. A quiet corner to quell his desperation. A coffee served by that nice Scottish lass who missed the islands.

'Working late again?' Roslyn would say, her forehead creased with concern.

'Got delayed,' he'd tell her, his heart pierced with anguish.

One evening, William bought a whole meal—haddock in parsley sauce—and sat near the window, chewing it slowly, the traffic sluicing along the wet road, families coming in, peeling off their coats. He tried not to think of Roslyn glancing at the clock, turning the oven to low, switching the radio on in case there'd been an accident. When he got home, he feigned illness, watched her spoon the casserole into a Pyrex dish, slide it into the fridge without a word.

William saw that the old phone box was gone, a potted tree where it once stood, near the entrance, like a sentry box. One winter, a thick slab of snow on its roof, he'd slipped inside, shivered as the coins dropped, dialled his own number. When he heard Roslyn's voice, he put down the receiver, pressed his forehead against the freezing glass until someone coughed outside, stepped back to let William stumble into the dark.

And that spring day, patches of yellow light on the hills, a queasy, wind-streaked sky. William had felt in his pocket for a coin, slowed the car once again. This time, if Roslyn answered, he would tell her. Try to explain that he could wait no longer. That he loved her but he had to go. Forget the drab chill of his office, this grey road, shepherd's pie on Tuesday nights, the clock ticking in the hall.

The phone rang on.

'Hello?'

Roslyn. William tried to speak, tried to form something from the jumble of his pain. Roslyn was silent for a long time, listening to him sobbing.

'Come home,' she said. He heard her gasp for breath. Never forgot it. 'We need to make plans.'

And he knew, then, they would go together. That she loved him enough to give up everything. To head south to a new life.

The rain had stopped. A brisk wind tossed the tops of the trees. William gripped the wheel. He'd go, head on to the village. The people in their old place are wonderful gardeners, his cousin told him. It's looking great. William smiled to himself. Roslyn would have loved that.

He rested his hand on the wooden box beside him, her ashes in a small brass urn inside. How he missed her.

'Let's get you home, my girl,' he whispered.

He turns the key. Outside, a newspaper tumbled across the car park, its pages gusting into the air, one sheet flapping its paper wings, landing, delicate as a bird.

Amanda O'Callaghan is an Irish/Australian writer. Her short stories and flash fiction have been shortlisted and awarded in multiple contests. Her collection, This Taste for Silence, was shortlisted for the Readings Prize for New Australian Fiction, and longlisted for the Edge Hill Prize in the UK. She lives in Brisbane.

5

WANTED: PREGNANT WOMAN SEEKS DUNNOCK, PARENTING EXPERIENCE PREFERRED

BY GILL O'HALLORAN

Sofie's pregnant, three months gone. She's just been promoted to maths lead, but her cells have divided and sub-divided like precocious scholars, without her oversight, and her maternal instinct is an untested equation, unsafe.

It cannot be.

She turns sideways to the mirror. Nipples are pinch purple, and now she spies those telltale blue-bruise veins, surfing the surface of her plumping breasts. She strokes them, the early light catching a gossamer of downy hair.

It is.

The next day the kids in class press in on her, a gaggle of beaks gaping wide for answers, *right or wrong?* It's not that simple, she says. She ignores them, preens herself behind the desk, purses her mouth at them if they approach. They learn to retreat before she can nip.

In the playground she observes the women, how they treat their offspring, fixes on Marsha; well-organised, petite but strong, she's seen her drive a car like a tank. She could easily manage more children; she's only got the one boy.

When Sophie's offspring is born she doesn't have to will herself not to bond, it's instinct. She doesn't name her fledgling, will not meet its half-blind eyes as it seeks an anchor. She ignores the breastmilk seeping through her tee-shirt, feeds it with bottles, pushes its seeking, flailing hands away from her.

On the day, she wraps it in a shawl, sees how lanugo covers its body; scrawny limbs, bulging head, muffled in dark fluff. When Marsha answers the door, she shows no surprise, lets her in. Sophie watches as her surrogate flits around the furniture, beady-eyed, busy, arranging the room just so. She places the infant on the carpet next to Marsha's 3-year-old, who startles; arms fly up, he starts to whimper, clenches pudgy fingers, and pushes them into the baby's face. Marsha doesn't blink, picks up the baby girl, and starts to coo, ignoring her son.

Only when Sophie has walked out the door, will she stand still on the lawn, look back, feel her head pound. One question presses in on her, gaping wide for an answer:

Will my child look at women in the street, wonder: is that my mother?

She boots the question out, holds her cradle-emptied arms to the sky, sniffs the air. And then she soars, perches in branches high above the careworn streets, opens her beak, and calls, a simple two-note triumph ringing out into the blue.

Cuck-oo.

Wanted: Pregnant woman seeks dunnock, parenting experience preferred by Gill O'Halloran © 2024

Gill's poetry book 'This Seven-Year-Old Walks Into a Bar' was included in the top 20 individual collections of 2009 by the Small Press Poetry Awards. She loves running poetry workshops but has only recently discovered the thrill of squeezing small stories into tight spaces. She has fiction published in Bath Flash Fiction Anthology 2024, Trash Cat Lit, Underbelly Press, Thin Skin. Find her on X @poetrypleases

6

AN UNLIKELY AWAKENING

BY GAYLE BEVERIDGE

The African violet on the sill, sorely in want of water, has wilted and its leaves drape limply over the edges of its blue plastic pot. Ivy hates seeing it so, but yet another night of wakeful sleeping has draped her in weariness. She keeps her seat, leans heavy against the table; mourns all that age has stolen from her and wallows in a pervasive indifference to life.

Plates stacked on open shelves in the corner kitchen are a constant reminder that she should eat. Her once shapely blouse hangs from her shoulders like an artist's smock, and only last week, for the third time this year, Ivy had to pierce another hole in her belt.

She picks up the remote and flicks on the TV. A talk show, three people on a couch all speaking at the same time, the words jumbling together and Ivy cannot pick them apart. A different channel, a young couple seeking to buy a house, champagne tastes on a beer budget; the homes they reject are mansions to Ivy. She sighs and tries the radio instead. A shock jock rudely shouting outrageous opinions, gathering ignorant fans who care little for facts. Every day the same meaningless drivel, the same long wait for the hours to pass.

Ivy sips her tea and stares past cracked paint and rotting wood, through a window frosted with dust. The sun is high; the day half over and nothing to show for it. Then 'THUNK!' A loud sound, a heavy sound, a sound with no business here. What was that? A car crash? A distant explosion? What?

She doesn't remember standing or spilling her tea over her trousers. She can see something flicking about in the dirt outside. A sparrow, on its back, throwing itself around, but still on its back. On the window is a patch where the dust is missing. 'No, no, no,' Ivy calls to no-one there. The bird is clearly in pain. What to do, what to do?

The sparrow stills. Will it get up? Perhaps it is dead now. Ivy watches, but she is not the only vigilant observer. The neighbour's cat is perched atop the paling fence, its hind legs crouched for the spring, its slitted yellow eyes greedy in anticipation. 'No, no, no,' Ivy calls in a voice worn soft, to a creature too wicked to pay her heed even if she could be heard.

Ivy grabs a tea-towel, fumbles with the door lock, and makes her way in rapid bursts of shuffles, into the yard. She flicks the tea-towel, and the startled cat slaps a paw at this chequered green and white assault. Twice more, Ivy flicks and twice more the cat slaps, before relinquishing its place and disappearing behind the fence.

Ivy goes to the sparrow and looks down at its unmoving body, its closed eyes, its tiny upended feet. She'll wrap the bird in the tea-towel and put it in the bin. She cannot bear to think the cat will have it, but when she kneels beside it, she sees the sparrow is breathing. She doesn't want to touch it, but it is alone here where it has fallen.

She folds the tea-towel, overlapping it once, twice, three times, into a tiny soft cushion. She sets it on the ground and with trembling hands gently lifts the bird and lays it on its make-shift bed. Indoors she tips her best shoes, the ones she wears to funerals, from their box. She makes air holes in the lid and carefully places the sparrow inside, away from light and noise. Is this the right thing to do? Ivy does not know, but if she were hurt, she would want to be in bed, in quiet solitude with the blinds closed.

Ivy puts the box on the shady end of the table and makes another cup of tea. She watches the box as she drinks, checks it when she has finished, and finding no change in the sparrow makes another cup of tea. Near on an hour passes, sipping tea and checking the box, until finally the sparrow looks back at her, trembling, but upright and alive. It doesn't move from its tea-towel bed, so Ivy closes the box again. She fills the lid of a small jar with water and grates some biscuit crumbs onto a slip of paper. She makes her offerings and by the time they are accepted and the bird returns to a lively state, the afternoon is ready to make way for evening.

Ivy takes her charge outside, places more water and biscuit crumbs on a rickety potting table, and carefully sets the sparrow beside them. A slight breeze ruffles its feathers and it hops one happy little hop. Then it is gone, flown off to somewhere else.

The dark hours that night are shorter than Ivy recently remembers them to be. She wakes, early enough for breakfast, with no recall of peering endlessly at the ceiling, of glances at a clock marking time that is reluctant to move on. She does recall as she sets the kettle to boil, that she had left the bird box on the table outside last night and goes to collect it before it blows away. To her surprise he is there, her little sparrow. At least she thinks it's him, cleaning up the biscuit crumbs. He looks at her for a second or two, after his meal, and again he is gone.

Ivy toasts a slice of bread, tops it with jam and washes breakfast down with a cup of tea. Then, with a whole day still ahead of her, she plans a trip to the supermarket, the first item on her list; birdseed.

An Unlikely Awakening by Gayle Beveridge © 2024

Gayle Beveridge writes because she loves it. It is her radiant red-sky sunset, her budding spring flowers. It is bird song and a long walk in the bush. Gayle is a past winner of the Boroondara Literary Awards. Her work has appeared in Award Winning Australian Writing, The Umbrella's Shade, Vegemite Whiskers and Mosaic. Gayle is passionate about writing, photography, sunsets, dogs, and chocolate and with Victoria's beautiful Bass Coast which she now calls home.

PART II

'THE HISTORY OF MANKIND IS THE INSTANT BETWEEN TWO STRIDES TAKEN BY A TRAVELLER.'

FRANZ KAFKA, THE THIRD OCTAVO NOTEBOOK, TRANSLATED BY ERNST KAISER AND EITHNE WILKINS

Today, I woke up as the Queen in Buckingham Palace. I smiled to myself, delighted of all that I could command. I could instantly imagine the terror I could avenge on those who had thwarted me in the past: the malicious boss, the menacing PE teacher... those brutal, narrowed eyes in her good-looking face trained just on me. I couldn't help but feel a twinge of otherness to her. She was a breathing honest-to-goodness human being.

I couldn't see myself in that human mirror. I try to catch my reflection in a pane of glass.

An 'exquisite corpse' micro-fiction from Bodleian Libraries' writing workshops

7

HOLD

FIRST PLACE PRIZE WINNER

BY ANDREW LANG

I remember you running faster than the other mums on sports day, I remember you saying, I'm not like the others I'm way out weird, I remember you saying, dry it up and put it away, never leave anything by the sink, I remember you singing on your guitar, oh the buzzing of the bees in the cigarette trees, I remember you saying, oh to be normal, anything to be normal, I remember thinking you'd go on forever.

I remember you saying I want you to have the things I never had, I remember you saying, go out with as many girls as you can, you learn something from everyone, I remember you shouted, But not that one, no, break up with her, now! I remember you loved the title of the book, Why Be Happy When You Could Be Normal? I remember you saying, these are the best days of my life, but I've found them so late, I remember you singing, freight train, freight train moving so fast.

I remember you sitting on your stool by the Aga with your dog on your knees, I remember your gentle hands when you touched animals, I remember your gentle hands on the back of Dad's neck when he was low, I remember you saying you'd lie awake at night thinking of all the stupid things you'd said, I remember you shouting, Oh my goodness if you could only hear yourself! I remember feeling angry when they looked down on you, I remember your loneliness, I remember you asleep in the afternoons with your glasses on and a book on your knees, Egyptian PE you called it, I remember when I said, you should get that cough looked at.

I remember reading in a Stuart Dybeck story, It was the first time I'd ever had the feeling of missing someone I was still with, I remember you drafting letters, the crossing out, the rewriting, the crossing out again, and then the final version, I remember you whispering, he'll fall apart when it happens and looking at Dad, I remember reading to you as you slept: a book called The Great Circle, I remember you saying, my life began the day you were born.

I remember I smashed a plate against the wall. I remember I tried to sleep in your bed but I felt afraid. I remember defrosting your beef stew. I remember your half-moon glasses all around the house. I remember your empty shoes. I remember forgetting the date it happened, was it the ninth, or was it the eleventh? I remember thinking, but how could I forget? And if I can forget that, then what else?

Andrew Lang is a writer and filmmaker who lives in London. His debut film, Sons of Cuba, won Best Documentary at the Rome

International Film Festival and Best Newcomer at the British Documentary Association Awards. He has written several screenplays, which various production companies are developing. He is new to the joys of flash fiction, and Hold is his debut publication.

8

ACCORDING TO WIKIPEDIA, MOST DAMSELFLIES EMERGE IN COOL, DAYTIME CONDITIONS

FINALIST

BY SHERRY MORRIS

Halfway through pegging out the laundry, Clara hears it—motorised *thuck-thuck-thuck-thuck-thuck*. She scans the horizon. Watches black spots grow in a steel-wool sky as her heart kickstarts. She drops the clothes pegs. Runs.

,

He'd plucked her from mundanity. In a whirlwind courtship, beguiled her with promises of an enchanted life set in a heather-draped land full of mirror-clear lochs and dark-chocolate Munro hilltops. Swept away by his adventurous tales and attention, Clara left her parents' suburban-beige home. Found herself set-down let-down in a draught-riddled farmhouse, caring for his elderly parents. Raised old-world right, she knew the rules: *Nice girls don't complain*.

,

She hurries along the thistle-laden path beside the drystone wall—a shortcut to the boutique hotel. With its immaculate landscaped grounds and grand manner, it's the posh part of the long-ago carved-up estate. The vast manicured front lawn is an ideal, if unexpected, place for helicopters to land. As they arrive the air pulsates. Deafens. Whirrs. Stirs something dormant, yet wild and impetuous within her.

,

Clara could only gawp the first time six sleek copters descended slowly, one by one, and landed in a precise perfectly choreographed V on the picturesque lawn, their round bodies brightly coloured in red, neon green or magenta. With their thin tails, bulbous bug-eyes and bladed wings, they remind her of the graceful dragonflies that dart and hover at lochans. But when the initial giant mechanical insect stilled, the hatch opened and a pilot leapt out.

Dressed in t-shirt and shorts, with sun-kissed skin, wide smile and white teeth, he appeared California-surfer carefree. As he shook hands with the genteel hotel owner who welcomed him and the rest of the Helicopter Club to their lunch and tea, Clara marvelled at the lifestyle of these high-flying men.

Later, with a mixture of envy and awe, she watched as each of these magical machines lifted effortlessly from its confined space in elegant 180° pirouettes. Trudging back to her duties, she wondered about the life of a Helicopter Club wife.

,

Now, two years on, compelled to come, Clara is once again on the lawn. She shadow-lingers pink-cheeked and breathless. When the tinted-glass eyelid of the huge dragonfly lifts and the pilot jumps out, her eyes remain on the creature.

The wish slices through her, deep. To skirr away. But not on the arm of a helicopter guy. She has shed her nice-girl naivety—gut-sense says Mrs Helicopter Club remains home alone too. Clara's desire is to solo-soar—find her own way, her own means—be the heroine of her own dreams this time. In the sudden silence, she exhales her wish into the air. Watches it float towards the exotic flying wonder. Its eyelid lowers. Clara catches its covert wink as it captures her wish. Her heart flutters. She has been acknowledged. Emboldened.

Whizzing back—she won't stay for the ache of take-off—her mind churns with preparations and possibilities. A sudden April breeze shifts to blustery gust, signalling a storm. Clara flits to the washing, lifts pegs. Laughs and waves as laundry flies away.

According to Wikipedia, Most Damselflies Emerge in Cool, Daytime Conditions by Sherry Morris © 2024

Originally from Missouri, Sherry Morris (@Uksherka & @uksherka.bsky.social) writes prize-winning fiction from a farm in the Scottish Highlands where she pets cows, watches clouds and dabbles in photography. She presents an online spoken-word radio show featuring short fiction with Inverness Hospital Radio. Many of her stories are influenced by her Peace Corps experience in 1990s Ukraine. Read more of her work at www.uksherka.com.

9

HERE IS A SLIDE

FINALIST

BY JAY MCKENZIE

Here is a slide on which your son sits and yells *mummy watch, watch me.* It is an orange plastic tube, not unlike the MRI scanner they pushed Steve into countless times before the end. Not that that tube was orange - more of a mortician-slab grey. This slide is going to make your son fizz with static, make him pop when he inevitably comes to touch your hand. *Ouchy,* he'll say. *We're electric,* you'll reply.

Here is an orange plastic slide standing in place of the metal one that used to ice over in the winter, burn your arse in the height of summer. A slide you tumbled from reaching for your sister's hand. It was so tall then, as things were before *health and safety gone mad,* and no spongey poured rubber to catch the fallers. *We are pioneers,* said your sister, but neither of you knew what that meant, only how delicious it was to leave at first light with a stick of Opal Fruits stuffed down your welly.

Here is a slide on which later, you will sneak a cigarette. You will push yourself into the mouth of the thing, holding the glowing tip like a baton in the hope that you don't drop ash and melt the plastic. There is already a bubbled scar on the top where an every-second weekend dad dropped a flaked finger of Regal while pretending he wasn't working hard to hold trembling ventricles together. You will hide in the gummy recess and hope that no-one sees you cry, then you'll spritz on some Clinique *Happy,* head back to your sister, folded into Steve's armchair while your son dozes in front of Peppa Pig.

Here is a slide that replaced a slide that replaced a dandelion-choked square of land. You remember it, or at least you think you do, but your sister says that you don't. *Before your time,* she says, and recalls broken milk bottles like shark teeth waiting in the grass to nibble up naughty children who throw rocks at the poor kids. *We were happy then*, she says, but her smile is too bright like wallpaper pasting over the hole that was hunger.

Here is a slide that replaced a slide that held you on an unsteady incline while a council estate boy pushed his fingers inside you. Your face was pressed into the cold metal, echoing your cries that were mistaken for moans. Those moans that followed you for the rest of Year 8 until some other girl did some other thing deemed *slutty* and everyone forgot about the wet gusset of your market stall underwear.

Here is a slide where, after slipping from the plastic maw on a midnight smoke you'll come face to face with a teenager who'll say *gis one of those* tilting a nod at your Marlboro Lights. You will be about to say no, but you'll catch a glint of an inert teardrop in the carroty glow of the park light. You will sit together, smoke another and she'll ask you if you've seen *The Beach.* You'll shake your head. Won't be able to remember when you last watched a film. It's an old one, she'll tell you. *There's this secret beach,* she'll say. *In Thailand. One day I'm gonna go there.*

Here is a slide where you'll bring your son again, remember that film. As he's sliding down, you'll think of that girl saying she'll go to Thailand one day and you'll remember pouring over holiday brochures with Steve, dreaming of a honeymoon you'd never be able to afford. You will remember twisting the cubic zirconia around your finger, and him saying *I'll get you a real one one day.*

Here is a slide that replaced a slide where you drank MD 20/20 with the year 11 boys. Where you threw up on your fake three stripes, and struggled to focus on your sister, arms folded, old in her teenage body saying *you have to come home, you've got to come now.* The slide that she pulled you up from while the boys jeered and she pulled your arm across her shoulder, wrapped her own around your waist and took you home to show you the broken light fitting she'd cut your mother down from.

Here is a slide where you will climb to the top, stare across the city of rust and bone at your feet, breathe in the choking perfume of dog shit and decay, wonder if this really is the best you can offer your boy. Here is a slide from which you will jump and feel yourself fly. *If I can catch the wind here,* you'll think, *then why not anywhere?* Your landing will be cushioned, you will bend your knees like they taught you in gymnastics back when you still thought you could be anything. You will return to your son and your sister, curled together on the Strawberry Shortcake sheets that both you and your sister have sweated, bled, cried on. You will flick through YouTube, find some clips of that impossible white, that unfathomable blue. Some singers you vaguely remember will sing to you about wanting to be taken there, to that secret beach on the other side of the world. You will look at the house, crumbling around you like pastry, wonder how much someone would be willing to pay for the old-man bones and stilted breaths trapped in the fibres. You will search Skyscanner for the price of three tickets to Bangkok. Wonder if the three of you can jump off the top of the slide together.

Jay McKenzie is the author of Mim and Wiggy's Grand Adventure (Serenade Publishing, 2023). Her work has appeared at or is forthcoming in adda, Unleash, Bath Flash Fiction Anthology, Flash Fiction Magazine, The Ulu Review, Reverie and other publications. Winner of the Exeter Story Prize and numerous others, she was shortlisted for the Exeter Novel Prize and the Commonwealth Short Story Prize. She is a nomadic Brit who currently lives on Jeju Island, South Korea with her husband, daughter and too many cardigans. Find her at www.jaymckenzieauthor.com or on Instagram @jay_writes_books.

10

LOST AND FOUND IN CLAPHAM

BY HELEN KENNEDY

She finds a baby on the Tube, pale and flimsy, wrapped in plastic. A small spiral circle inked onto the back of its hand. Blue breath. She feels for a pulse, slow, suboptimal and decides to put it into her rucksack. She knows about abduction; it has all happened before.

Clapham Common is damp and drowsy with rain. The trees overhang, turning yellow. Unseasonal. The sweet smell of decay. A group of hooded lads congregate to smoke under the pavilion. She keeps her head down, hopes the baby won't make a sound. The streets are empty and exhausted, the black shine surfaces full of abandoned cars and empty electric buses. No one thought it would happen this quickly. Along Abbeville Road she keeps to the left side, in the shade of walls and hedges. Gail's bakery used to have a long queue, but now there is a small slit cut in the door, where a hand delivers flat loaves of sourdough and polenta cake. The shop windows barricaded.

She'd always dreamed of a life in the city, the suburbs stretching like elastic into empty spaces. The wide open common, green, and resourceful. She ran rings around the mown tracks and drank coffee at Peartree café. Life was mellow and certain. Miles had a job at the Phoenix, curating films, and art exhibitions. She knitted textiles and sold them online, and at small community markets. The flat was at the end of a long lease, shabby and swollen with damp plaster. Window frames that rattled. They spent weeks sanding and scouring, painted surfaces scraped clean from neglect. The landlord raised the rent, but it felt like it was a forever home, a place to grow.

She lays the baby on the kitchen table, carefully unwraps it and puts her face to its bud lips. The small rise and fall of its chest and the smell of its sweet milky breath. The baby is dressed in a soft cotton romper, it has pale blue eyelids, and peach cheeks. She makes a bottle of milk and feeds it in the crook of her arm. She has to try; she has no choice.

They'd given up on fertility, the endless temperature charts and injections, slow months when the blood wouldn't stop, and she was sick and tired of trying. Miles made light of it, they were young, he said and unlikely parents so soon. But something inside her already knew that a child would one day be hers. She used to walk Venn Street Market watching mothers and noticed who held and who didn't hold their babies. Tight knit in slings and held to hard breasts to feed, hidden in cardigan and coats. Outside Ground, coffee drinking mothers sat at a circle of tables. It was casual. Confidently cool. No one knew what was coming next.

The baby stirs. It stretches and arches, raising both balled-up fists to the side of its head. It feels dreamy to hold, inconsequential. She knows that Miles will want to know where she found it, what she proposes to do and she will show him her cupboard supplies, powdered milks, and nappies, follow on jars and tins of food for weaning. She's been planning this for months. Making a future for them both. She'll have to find a way of keeping the baby placated, Mrs Murtagh lives upstairs and the noise travels through thin walls and bare floorboards. She hears her sometimes dragging her old feet up the stairs, hauling herself to the landing.

Her childhood in the west of Ireland had been filled with wild abandon, hazy summers in the thick of fields and swinging on ropes over rivers. Her mam never knew where they were, untethered to their hedonism. She remembers the feather tailed ponies that roamed the hillsides, the purple haze of heather. The air that tasted of the sun. She hadn't wanted to grow up fast; but nothing lasts. Sometimes the life we dream of isn't possible and we only have what's left.

It's already dusk when she hears Miles' key in the door, she hears him throw his bag to the floor, kick off his shoes. The baby is swaddled in a pale-yellow blanket. She can't let him see it so soon. So, she tucks it with the sofa cushions and heads to the hob, gets the wok nice and hot to stir fry beef and bok choy, furikake and miso noodles, a splash of sauce. Miles complains that the tube has been shut down, an incident with ticker tape and a police dog search. Urban enforcement officers combing the station platforms. No one saying the word, outcast.

They've already drunk two glasses of sake before she shows him the baby. 'Not again,' Miles says. 'For fuck's sake Alisa, why can't you follow the rules.' But there are no rules when you've already given up so much. She has love to give and a baby to give it to.

They sleep in separate rooms, the baby is warm and fuzzy in the cocoon of her blanket, she knows that Miles isn't asleep next door, but she can't reach him. The next morning, he has left his keys on the table, a note that says, 'give it up.' But the expression of love is a transformative process.

She scours the news on SM. No mention of the find. It's a secret, shared with everyone, and no one. She wants to be a mother and can't understand the subversive propaganda of population containment. The restrictions. No one can explain where the rules came from.

She holds the baby in her arms, stares out at the sky falling into molten layers of uncertainty. Holding onto the world she knew, for what she might have been. She calls them all baby. It is all she can do.

Helen Kennedy is a writer of short stories and flash fiction, published by the Brick Lane Short Story Prize, the Bristol Prize and by Fly on the Wall Press. Her flash fictions have been published by NFFD anthology 2024, the Oxford Flash Fiction Prize, reflex and Flash 500. She has recently completed a debut novel. @helenkennedywrites

11

LIGHT PRESSURE

FINALIST

BY MICHAEL MURPHY

More prayer than song, more plea than prayer, an a cappella shrill thrust headlong into the night. Before the light of day, a bird in Brixton calls and falls sharply silent, its lungs unheeded in shrunk surrender. Lena listens. Palm cradling cheek, thumb tucked behind lobe, the back of her hand against pillow. On the cusp of sleep she whispers, 'It's not a nightingale.'

Lena will wake before the day that is not. She'll stir soup on the hob and sing Polish lullabies. The twist of the doorknob a needle-across-vinyl shriek. And he'll smell. Filthy and fertile. Like rain burning off a dirty street.

Khalid will ditch the hi-viz, smile, and kiss her naked nape. Crack wise. Warm his chords with Kronenbourg. He'll audition his voices; the lover, the paranoid, the leave me the fuck alone. She'll sip chamomile as he pulls himself apart on the lino. Limbs flailing. Best not to touch. Just leave him be. Sometimes Earl Grey.

Lena knows. Ritual is a blanket that keeps you warm. A flammable blanket that keeps you warm.

Pre-dawn birdsong will lift Khalid from the kitchen floor. Unravel his contortions, cradle him, carry his broken body upward to be laid prone by Lena. It is only then that she'll find sleep. She'll fall fast in the knowing that this is not the night that creaking stairs go silent. When it comes – when day breaks without the anxious dark of shuffling footfall – she will whistle softly in bed and wait. She will whistle and wait. She will whistle as morning turns to afternoon and afternoon to night. She will whistle until the rush of wind through her upturned tongue intertwines with the robin's winter plea.

Lena isn't wrong. She struggles with conjugation. Khalid isn't here, of course. But, he's here, of course. Khalid is not here. He will be. Here. Soon Khalid will be here.

He'd be happy with chicken from a tin. Prefer it, even. To carve flesh from carcass, roll it between fingers, to let her face linger over a steam of broth and bone is her shy subterfuge.

A pink blade had for nothing at Oxfam. Everyone knows you don't butcher with ceramic. Lena knows. She carves and picks. And picks. Carves and picks and eats. Khalid won't eat dark meat. She swallows the moist bits and a rosy chip of razor. Sets it on its course. A spanner in the terminal tick tock. Having a thing inside you that's not you. Deciding. The morning may come or a tug of the moon, a sharp song, and sleep.

'It would've killed you,' Khalid had said. It.

Would have. Such certainty. An anchor stitch that keeps us bound to the ground. That keeps innards in and the outer out. Knowing is not knowing. The stitch will pop. The stars will fall. Gravity's grip will loosen, and we'll be set adrift in a never-ending night.

Soup at a simmer, Lena makes her way upstairs.

Next to the dresser, the 35 flashes fluorescent outside the bedroom window. Twelve-minute intervals. The upper deck is never empty. Hoodie, hoodie, hijab. Headphones on. Eyes low. Cameos rolling, rolling by.

Khalid is at the Junction. He bounces between touts, numb to the shuffle, and on the 35 it's a tap-tap and scrum to the top to fight for a front row. From here he can see. Nobody gives a fuck if you crack a can. If they do, they're well behind you. Eyes ahead. But they give a fuck, Khalid. They do. They see you. Know you.

Lena knows. At 15km/h, a passing glance can't be had with a wave from a darkened flat. And was it even a wave? A raised palm. A start. She keeps the lights on now. Off and on. Her gyrations fully illuminated. The red-tasseled lamp dancing with the stomping of feet and clapping of hands.

At Clapham Common, Khalid watches young money at play. It ogles and snogs and considers the cinema.

Bare backs are exposed at Rookery Road where shiny things lounge on the lawn.

At the T, Brixton's killing kings and filling bins with bones of curried goat.

Before Gresham, what happens happens. Ginger's taking the piss, Khalid. Over your shoulder. Backseat ginger. He's taking the piss.

Lena's delirium accelerated by all-caps. BUS TROUBLE HUNGRY puts her to thinking. Puts her in motion. Hungry.

At Western Road, the defenestration of Khalid Ali. Through the rear door. Rousted from the daily drowse to cheers. Nothing as rapturous as the pimple popped. The splinter freed.

Khalid scrambles for footing in the glare of probing headlights, slings a bicycle from the curb to block the bus's advance. He dissolves into bright white. Above him, Lena's silhouette strobes weightless – untethered – its contours a quarter rest.

In the glow, Khalid knows. He's done something unforgivable. He's done something. Amends will be made when a name is put to the charge. The sentence served. There's only one of him now. Clearly outlined. Hungry. Gripped by a guilt that twists. Ex nihilo. Twists until he sings. With an upward glimpse at Lena, a whispered scream.

Passengers grumble and jeer. Alone but not alone. Spotlit by false luminosities, we sing our own sad songs. No one sings along. No one knows the words. Why would they? How would they? What do they know? Bugger all, that's what.

Lena knows. Nighttime south of the river is a perverted reverie. The pleading robin's lie of streetlamp half-light. Foxes toppling bins to evensong of unheard choristers, wailing like babies, wandering free and unmoved by passerby who have lost their way home.

Michael Murphy's fiction has featured in the Notre Dame Review, Squawk Back, Sunspot, and MONO, his non-fiction in the Asheville Citizen-Times, his write-for-hire pablum in myriad feeds, screens, and pulp. While living in London, Michael wrote an award-winning satirical column for the Hampstead Village Voice.

12

THE EXPERIENCE MACHINE

BY LOUISA MCDONALD

In the 1974 book 'Anarchy, State, and Utopia', the philosopher Robert Nozick came up with the thought experiment of the Experience Machine. The question it asks is this: if you could go into a machine that perfectly simulated a happy life, much happier than your life, and spend the rest of your days in that machine, would you?

It's been almost a whole day since I lost Mother to the Machine.

It was an unpopular idea when it first came out. Everybody saw it on the news, and everybody said the same thing: no way. No way would I go into the Machine. I want my own life, the real life, no matter how unbearable it gets.

It is 2091. January. I step into the cold morning air. Each day, it seems that the number of figures clad in coats gets smaller. I board the tram to work, watching the houses flicker by. The poor souls wrapped in ragged scarves huddle together and whisper audibly to each other.

I'm saving up, one says. In four months' time, if I'm careful with my spending, I'll be able to buy a Machine.

I'm just waiting for the kids to leave home, mutters another. I'm sick of it all. As soon as Jocelyn graduates, I'll be getting a Machine. I can't take it anymore.

I slip in my earbuds to drown out their chatter. I can't take it anymore either.

When the Machine first got released, only the very rich could afford one. It was on the front page of Forbes, with smiling billionaires singing its praises. We all dismissed it as a passing fad. Such a ridiculous idea, and far too expensive. Besides, who would want something like that anyway? But they made more and more of them, and with each passing month, the price of the Machine went down. Soon, most well-to-do people could afford one. Strangely enough, once they could afford to buy one of their own, the antipathy that people harboured towards the Machine began to dwindle.

I arrive at work to even more empty desks than yesterday. The faces of the workers are ghostly pale, except for the dark circles around their eyes. I sit at my desk and check my watch. Eight hours to go. I will not talk to anyone; I will not drink the watery coffee from the vending machine; I will not take a break for lunch. I will spend the day doing what I usually do: writing up what they want me to write up on the website. The website changes every day. I couldn't even really tell you what it's for. But today, I do not wish to think of anything but my work. I especially do not want to think of Mother in the Machine.

When you go into the Machine, you are, of course, fitted up

with a feeding tube. It'll keep you alive until your heart stops beating. There is no recorded difference between a regular human lifespan and a lifespan in the Machine. In fact, the Machine probably gives you a slightly longer life. Once you're in the Machine, you immediately forget that you ever went in there. You live in the Machine as if it were the life you'd always had. It feels like real life, but all your wants, dreams, hopes, and desires, can finally come true. You'll never know pain or worry again. You won't even know that this digital dream isn't reality. And you can do it all from the comfort of your own home, as the relentless adverts for the Machine on billboards beside the road always insist.

Mother would always heave a sigh whenever we drove past one of those billboards. She would say, Stuff and nonsense, stuff and nonsense!

But back then, Mother still had hope in her eyes and laughter in her voice.

As more and more people left the real world and plugged into the Machine, the quality of life for those of us who remained got lower. There were hardly enough people to keep the wheels of the world turning. The Internet still worked, and the online world was probably more functional than the real one, but it was mostly run either by robots or by underpaid workers whose souls had been drained from their eyes. In my office, we cannot afford heating anymore, even in the depths of winter. I huddle into my wool coat. My fingertips are stiff from the cold. Nonetheless, I type away and carry on typing.

With the world wilting away, buying a Machine has become

the aspiration for everyone. All the workers in my office say, I'm saving up, I'm saving up, I'm nearly there, we'll have Machines for the whole family by August, I'm telling you!

People often ask me when I will be able to afford a Machine.
I say, I can already afford one.
Then, what are you waiting for? they ask.
It would be useless to try to explain to them that I don't want one. They'd never understand.

Mother used to understand. We used to be on the same page about all of this. But there came a time when her eyes would grow sadder and sadder each day. I would bring her cups of tea, ask her what was wrong, she would just shake her head and say, Nothing, darling, it's nothing.

When I called Mother's house this morning and a strange voice answered, I was worried something had happened to her. The voice explained to me not to worry, that he'd just been here to install the Machine in Mother's house. I felt a drop in my chest. I told him to wait, that I would be right there, but he said there was no need, Mother was already safely plugged in to the Machine. He sounded triumphant, as if he'd done his good deed for the day.

All I could think was: if only I had been a better son.

Louisa McDonald recently graduated from Oxford University with a Masters in Modern Languages, having studied German and Philosophy at the University of St Andrews at undergraduate level. She is interested in how philosophy and literature can come together and has previously written philosophical stories for ST.ART Magazine, a St Andrews-based arts magazine. She also occasionally writes in other languages and in 2021 won the writeAUT prize for her short story in German. She is a keen photographer, and you can follow her photography account on Instagram: @louisa_photographs

13

THE EXTEMPORAL HABERDASHERY

BY DEREK JON DICKINSON

He called me on the phone, one of the few people who could summon me. I wanted to make my way there, to see him, his purple-bright intelligence, his Kempsford-parish mien, which was washed last time by a severe light.

Fishing with crampons on the ice-severed Two Harbor's pier. Sleet scratching his stubbled face. An unleveraged, centrifugal figure, self-emancipated from convention. Boyish in anything he wore: a cigarette or frayed fisherman's sweater, tailored suit or an Irish paddy-cap. One of two boys, raised divorced-suburban-poor. Humble despite himself—his broad swimmer's torso, his thick, wind-tossed hair. My friend, with the vintage red motorcycle he bought at a garage sale. My friend who, unbeknownst, absorbed the thoughts, the hours and minutes of others. Who moved to Duluth for college, remained for its art.

I don't mean the city is known for its art museums, though it has some, but the place itself has art—confluence of pit-mined taconite and sagaciously-wild conifers; of syllabi-strict disciplines and Lake Superior's ornery sea-antlers.

I check my watch—past noon. Before the visit I would need a drink. Not a drink, really, but courage. Not courage, but the need to conjecture, or prepare. Not that, either. I don't know what, really. Call it a strange supplanting. An evasion, I suppose, or simple distraction.

Exegesis (of myself): loafers, exiting a train, tattered passport—preferring arguments, apologies, anything that's moving. Alcohol, schizophrenia of pleasures. I was staying away from that. Walking.

I walk a lot. The torn pages of Duluth's sea-allusive streets; Canal Park juts from the mainland, cobbled strand of hotels and tourist shops. Home of the famous aerial lift-bridge—gate of Superior Bay, chopping-off the weather like a guillotine.

Waterfront antique store, a little bell chimes when I open the door. I have found, that besides the impractical (and expensive) pleasures of travel, that this—the dissociative, or associative (depending upon one's needs)—browsing-regimen can satisfy—temporarily at least—one's peripatetic needs.

Thus, I browse, instead of drink. Rarely with the impulse to pick anything up; except to feel its weight. Old is so much heavier—old iron, old glass. And admittedly, old memories.

Unabated musings, shelf after shelf. Orphaned light pirouetting in blue-faceted perfume-bottles; crockery-jugs of booze too old to drink—desiccated glue and labels falling off. I was never a vodka-shaky tremoring drunk, but a closet pleasure-seeker; an astute drinker—college educated, rumored erudite. Placating my body in order to free the mind, and so-on. Beer in the evenings, mostly. The low alcohol, high water content being both throttle and brake.

I check my watch again, its blind hands groping the shims of precedent. Here in the antique store, I can loiter as long as I want. Who knows what memories or sympathies have struck me. Who knows which of these items has vexed me. Northerners, known for our impassive qualities. As long as I look insipidly cheerful, or insipidly foreboding, no one will bother me.

Hours pass. My watch, a Swiss automatic; escapement heartbeat, wound by the chaos of my wrist. My friend bought me this watch. Used. With his normal prescience, had no idea I needed it until he gave it to me.

My good friend. That last time I saw him, his eyes wild as the sea. Silhouetted on the icy pier; his metal crampons' serrated teeth, gnawing the ice as he shifted, casted; into the indifferent cold. The lure, beveled and silver, with the heft of lead.

In the speech-bending wind, trying to read the poem of my friend, the complex verse of a gusted person. The flash of the lure, the unspooling monofilament.

Antique store, allegorical mirror. Each item, a used decision. A parting of money, its requital of labor. The perishables are omitted, the socks and the underwear. And the food, of course, missing from the tin. Though, if something does remain, it rattles.

And myself perishable, curious what remains after wont has abdicated. We swarm estate sales, busy as flies, doing our part to decompose the life.

I look at my watch—five o'clock. I really must go. To see my friend. Who's in pain about something. I could fill his sails with literature's brusque winds. I could stop at the rare bookstore and bring him some poems. His high rhetoric and perfunctory vicissitudes; comportment poised like a cello—perfectionist, highly-irritable.

My friend's occasional trips to the strip-bar. Caveated in plain sight—jazz-club by day, lap-dances by night. Huddled on the edge of waves, our moral periphery.

Not an ogler, my friend, but a sipper. Would be just as

likely to interview her as to extract any pleasure. Invite her to a movie, buy her something within his modest means. All the while, looking her in the eye, asking nudely-incongruent questions—*Tell me, love, what accent would a man acquire if he spent an entire life on the pleated, manuscript sea?*

His self-allayed appetites, there's no desperation in him, no hurry for conclusion. It's because of this, this guileless confusion, why so many fall in love with him.

I could bring him a bottle of The Famous Grouse, something useful. These are the friendships I value most, where I make a plan then fear its fruition.

Exiting the antique store. In the chilled air. Walking.

There's a light on. He's inside. Through the wavy glass I see his silhouette. My soles scraping the gritty, cement steps. I arrive at the top and pause; adjust my scarf, brush snow off my woolen coat.

Thumbing the pages of our friendship; his curated presence, placed like a bookmark. Just before I knock, I tilt my head.

The most powerful moments of the liturgy are the interstices. The moments just after and just before; when the pastor motions his congregation to stand, and the wooden pews slightly shift; as the selves are set down, and the fabrics and the forgiveness and the hymnals, lift.

Derek Jon Dickinson is a writer and photographer living in Minnesota, United States. His writing has appeared or is forthcoming in Naugatuck River Review, Spoon River Poetry Review, The Manhattan Review, Dunes Review, Cordite Poetry Review (Australia), The MacGuffin and others. His waterfowl photography has been published by Ducks Unlimited.

14

IT'S JUNE IN KENTUCKY, AND BOB'S TRUCKING THROUGH ON I-65

BY COLE BEAUCHAMP

He rolls down the window and the night air hustles in, a heady mix of manure and tobacco that fits the song on the radio: Mama, don't let your babies grow up to be cowboys. Waylon and Willie sound good even rattling out of the Mack's podunk speakers.

Bob chomps on some Twizzlers, swigs A&W through a paper straw that's turned to mush. Maisie. Their clapboard house he built from the foundation up. The smell of mint and basil she grew from seed scenting their bedroom. Her gasp when their rhythm hits just right. The catch in her voice when he leaves, 'Don't you miss me?' She's always on him now to take that job at Pete's, says she wants to start a family.

The tires of his semi thrum on the asphalt. Now Loretta Lynn is on with *Don't come home a-drinkin*. He sees his father, the corded muscles of his neck, his mother wailing, 'Why why why?' After his dad left, Bob had years of clanking her empties into the garbage cans while she cursed out his string of women, though that wasn't what she said. Two syllables, who-ers.

Maisie doesn't get it. Bob's always alone, don't matter if he's at the garage or a thousand miles away. He can't give her what she wants. But staying away don't mean playing away. He's not his dad.

Up ahead, a sign for Bert's Travel Plaza, diesel about ten cents a gallon cheaper than he's seen since Birmingham. The engine whines as he downshifts. The air-brakes whistle. He fills up and takes a stroll through the truck stop to stretch his legs. Strip lighting bounces off two-liter bottles of Coke, bags of cheese popcorn and potato chips, an entire aisle of beer. T-shirts, stuffed animals, fridge magnets that say, 'Bourbon: Kentucky horsepower.' An adult section with blow-up dolls and porn.

He catches a whiff of steak and eggs from the 24-hour restaurant.

The thirty-something waitress has frizzy hair and a warm smile. 'Well hey handsome.' She blows a pink bubble and snaps it back.

He laughs. 'Hey yourself.' At this time of night, flirting helps pass the time.

He eyes the board. 'Steak any good?'

She winks. 'Mooing just yesterday.'

Bob sits at the counter and polishes off the $8.99 steak and egg special. The waitress, Michelle, tells him about her twelve-year-old son, her divorce from a man sneakier than a junkyard dog, not a red cent of alimony. 'I see you wear a ring.' Her voice is wistful as she studies his hand. 'Lucky girl, having a man who knows how to listen.'

He shifts on his stool. 'You like country music?'

'I like Taylor Swift.'

'She ain't country.'

Michelle crosses her arms. 'True or false: that little girl started her career in Nashville.'

'Did she?' Bob frowns. He's sure that blond-maned girl is a pop star, all legs and lip gloss.

'Yeah. Give her some credit. She's been writing her own songs since she was fourteen.'

Bob purses his lips. 'There ya go.'

A few truckers come in, arguing about whether the Chiefs or Bears will win the game, looking for him to join in but Bob just smiles and looks away.

A bone thin girl hovers in the doorway, shivering in a miniskirt and low-cut top. Her face looks ten years older than her body.

Bob looks away. Lot lizards are an occupational hazard – selling or hitching, sometimes thieving.

Michelle motions the girl into a booth and pours her a cup of coffee.

When she's back, Bob says, 'Doesn't that make it worse, giving 'em something for nothing?'

Michelle shakes her head. 'Little enough that girl's been given.'

The Bears fan calls out, 'Hey hon, come on over here, got something you'll like.' He leans back and rubs his crotch.

Mating and sex, predator and prey. Bob's glad his wife is tucked up at home. He wonders what it's like to be a nine to five guy, to coach Little League and go to church on Sundays. He shakes his head. What he can take pride in is providing for Maisie. Keeping his word. Being faithful.

He hears that catch in Maisie's voice again and stands to settle the bill. 'Well, you keep safe then.' He gives Michelle a twenty, tells her to keep the change.

'You sure?' She squints up at him, the fluorescent lights showing smudged mascara, lipstick that's bled into the creases of her lips.

'Little enough you've been given, I bet.'

Michelle reaches up and pulls him forward. Her lips are soft on his cheek. 'Bless you.'

She smells of fried food and coffee, but her hair holds the scent of strawberries. For an awful moment, Bob feels his cock stiffen. He wants to wrap his fingers in her berry-scented hair, bury his imperfections and sorrow into her forgiving body.

He mumbles goodbye, afraid to meet her eyes in case the answer is yes.

Outside the air stinks of petroleum and exhaust. He shakes himself like a dog that's been in the river too long. All these hours on the road, the truckers and that prostitute, it's all messing with him. He's not that kind of man.

Maisie. Her coppery hair against the pillow. Her green eyes boring into his, arms wrapped around his back. Maisie. His pulse steadies.

Climbing up the metal stairs into the cab, he grimaces at the old Whopper wrappers, empty Twizzler and Milk Dud packets, flat pop. He gathers it up and chucks it into a nearby garbage can.

Back in the driver's seat, he waits for the glow plugs. Maybe Maisie's right. Maybe he won't know until he tries. The orange of the glow plug light fades. New air in, old air out, the compression of pistons, heat. That spark of ignition and he's off.

He swings the Mack out of the parking lot, joins I-65 North. Maybe it wouldn't be so bad, that garage? The look on Maisie's face might just be worth it.

It's June in Kentucky, and Bob's trucking through on I-65
by Cole Beauchamp © 2024

Cole Beauchamp (she/her) is a queer writer based in London. She was in the Wigleaf Top 50 2024, a Best Microfictions 2024 nominee, and has been shortlisted in the Bridport, Bath and WestWord prizes for flash fiction. Her stories have appeared in New Flash Fiction Review, The Phare, trampset, Citron Review and others. She lives with her girlfriend and has two children. You can find her on Twitter at @nomad_sw18

PART III

'THERE REMAINS THE INEXPLICABLE MASS OF ROCK.'

PROMETHEUS, KAFKA, THE COMPLETE SHORT STORIES, TRANSLATED BY WILLA AND EDWIN MUIR

Today, I woke up on a pile of ashes. I sparked with all the power in me. I feel my body warm up a bit, but a spreading soreness goes through. My head is spinning. I try to focus on the red roses, flowers he gave me before he left for his film shoot in Miami 2 days ago. How sweet they smell. Psychologists tell us how smell contains memories, brings back moments into the imagination. Sweet and bitter. *Is the survival skill obtained through trauma or is it innate in all of us?* Questions build in a blind panic. What could I do? Who could I call? Was it just me or was this happening to others? I decided to risk looking in the mirror. Aaarghhh!

An 'exquisite corpse' micro-fiction from Bodleian Libraries' writing workshops

15

AMUSEMENT-PARK DAD

FINALIST

BY SLAWKA G. SCARSO

To the interviewer on daytime television, the man says love is uncountable. It's not a sum. It's not a geometric set. It's limitless, boundless. If you feed it, it grows, like an exponential curve, a logarithmic curve. The interviewer makes a joke about being a mathophobe. The man tells the interviewer that some people can hardly love themselves, and some can hardly love one person. 'I had love for more, what's wrong with that?'

At home, his daughter watches the recorded show. She wonders about the relativity of time. About the two fast hours when Mum called the handyman to change the front door lock. Packed Dad's suitcases. Left them on the front porch and slammed the doorbell with a hammer before Dad came home from his weekly *business trip* because she knew he would stamp his finger on the now-shattered bell. Her mother knew him well, though clearly not well enough. *To the interviewer, the man says he didn't break any law. Technically, it wasn't like he was married twice. And what about all the people out there having affairs? Why be so hypocritical?*

Until six months ago, time was slow. Summer dragged on.

She spent nights counting mosquitoes, and days reading and playing by herself, but mostly dozing and watching TV. She dreamt of being old enough to take her family on holiday, since they never took her. Maybe Disneyworld. She thought of searching for ways for children to make money fast and found her dad's personal computer. She tried several plausible passwords. When their Basset Hound barked, she wrote Otto and then her birthday. She was in. *But this was more than an affair, the interviewer implies, while the audience claps. And yes, maybe you were married only to one wife, but still, you must admit it's a little unconventional. And it's not like anyone was aware, or were they?*

The man shakes his head and replies that while it lasted, nobody ever accused him of neglecting them. That came later.

The daughter never got to the browser. Instead, she found a folder in her dad's computer. It said Disneyworld, the irony of it all. But they had never been. They were meant to go, many times, but something always came up. The folder's info said there were fifty-two photos inside. She opened it. And there was her dad, at Disneyworld. He looked just like he looked in the photos on the mantelpiece, and on the wall by the stairs. His wide smile, almost always bursting into laughter. And next to him, not her, not her mum, but another woman, and another girl sitting on his shoulders. Time froze, and then it melted, like her voice calling *Mum! Mum!* before she pointed at the folder and then, together, they found the others too: Disneyland, Legoland, Seaworld... All featuring her dad's wide smile and different women, different children all younger than her.

What I don't get is how you managed the holidays. Christmas? Surely that must have been hard? The man says 'For that, you'll have to read this', *and takes the book sitting next to him on the studio sofa. He shows it to the camera, holding it in front of his heart and beams. His face is on the cover. The title says Amusement-Park Dad in Disney font.*

In the future, she'll learn the book was written by a ghostwriter. Her therapist will suggest she tries to contact her half-siblings. She'll learn finding excuses is much easier than loving. She'll learn that her mood can have so many swings that no logarithmic curve can describe it as well as a rollercoaster. Eventually, she'll learn to flatten the peaks and soften the lows. When her Dad tries to contact her, she will send him an image of two parallel lines.

Slawka G. Scarso has published several books on wine in Italy and works as a copywriter and translator. Her words have appeared in Mslexia, Gone Lawn, Ghost Parachute, Fractured Lit and Scrawl Place among others. She was shortlisted for the 2023 Bridport Flash Award, the 2023 Oxford Flash Fiction Prize and the 2024 Bath Short Story Award. Her debut novella in flash "All Their Favourite Stories" is available from Ad Hoc Fiction. She lives in Italy. You can find her on X as @nanopausa and on www.nanopausa.com

16

INHERITANCE

RUNNER-UP FOR THE OXFORD PRIZE

BY BRIDGET JOHNS

We bury her on a Thursday. It would have been better on God's own day, Pa says, like Grandmother might need help telling up from down. Ma says it's better we do it quick so's she doesn't linger. That it'd be just like her to make trouble, 'cause she never knew how to stay out o' anyone else's business.

I just wish we weren't buryin' her at all.

The whole village streams down from the head of the valley when we carry her from the church, gathering in the harbour to bear witness. All the fishermen come, the farmers and the shepherds. The lord does, too, down from his manor. He looks the same as any of 'em, doffing his cap to her.

There's not a single missing face. That never happens 'cept for Mass, and it's got the same sort of hush, everyone in their best with their hair slicked back, hopin' that if they keep their palms together it'll hide the sin on 'em.

They're stupid for it. God never smote nobody when Donal got Mary round in the belly then pretended he didn't know her from Eve, but Grandmother took her hand and walked to his door, and a week later they were married. She never missed a thing, not even death.

When the procession reaches the pier, Pa loads the body into our boat, the shroud all grey and small, made out of fur and sealing her up tight like a catkin. Then he sails out far enough that she won't wash back to shore.

The villagers drain away after her, going back to the grindstone like the world hasn't ended. A couple of the two-faced ones give their best wishes to Ma, but the rest are honest enough to say nothing. I feel their eyes on me through the way she won't stop straightening my shawl. They'll be gossiping about the lack of wake no doubt, the unnaturalness of a sea burial, about what I'll do with her dead and no formal apprenticeship to my name. How I might have to settle down and join the rest of them respectable folk. But what kind of man would take me?

The questions nip my heels as I shake Ma off and pick my way out past the harbour, scrambling a path over the rocks until my feet hit shingle. My own scrap of beach, where the waves break their backs on the cliffside and the rocks shield against the headland. No eyes to see me here, no words to cut. As soon as I'm hidden from the docks, it all comes off. My bonnet first, then my shoes, my shawl lost to the wind.

There's a dead gull washed up today. It hangs out of a rock pool, all broken down to feathers and gristle, with two other birds squarin' off for the entrails. They snap and tussle until the victor hoists them into the sky, with a proud air like Ma wears sometimes after getting the last word.

She's won for good this time, but I don't know where that leaves me, little birdy in the middle.

The seals are out in the bay as usual, haulin' themselves onto their big flat rock so they can roll their bellies to the sky. I got nowt for them today, but they keep on watching all expectant, just as bad as everyone else. I stand there, ignoring them, letting the waves come until I am wet through, nothing left but cold and sand and salt.

Grandmother always said I'd find her in the ocean, but I close my eyes and feel nothing. It were her that brought me here the first time, something in her eyes all halved to see me clambering around on the rocks and running in the surf, the seals letting me tickle the big dark flat of their fur. She never got her own feet wet, just said her swimming days were done.

When I asked Ma what that meant she got all pinched lookin' and started mutterin' about sin. They rowed for weeks on end 'til I thought I'd never see Grandmother again - but no-one else would watch me while Ma worked, so she won that one. I only saw 'em at it worse when Grandmother knew she were dyin' and Ma wouldn't countersign the will. There was no safe quarter then, the air all sharp with words nobody was sayin'.

Grandmother never gave up a fight in her life except the one for me. Ma just had this way of gettin' under her skin. I asked her about it once, and she laughed and said Ma had too much of the land in her to let her bend. Then she looked at me and touched a thumb to my nose and said, but the water always finds a way, eh?

She kept mutterin' that on her deathbed too, wrapping my hands in her fur shroud and making me repeat it, her black eyes big like she wanted me to read a secret out of 'em.
One of the seals barks, returning me to my body. The tide is at my waist now, the light fadin'. They'll notice I'm gone soon. Then Ma's hands will be on my shoulders, and I know in my bones that I'll never come back here again.

The seal barks again sharper this time. They're all still watching me, waiting for me. All-knowing, cow-bright eyes, deep like the surface of still water. They're like hers were, like mine are, just set into a different face, and I understand, suddenly, what she was trying to tell me.

I see her shroud for the second skin that it was.
The village lights sit cradled by the valley, cascading down the hillside. I think about how water travels through rock on its way back to the ocean, picture my Grandmother's coat in my hands.

Then I turn my back on the headland and give myself to the sea.

Bridget Johns lives in Oxfordshire working for a charity by day and writing things by night. She loves sci-fi, fantasy, and all things messy about human relationships. Her short story, Pandora's Box, was shortlisted by the Aurora Prize for Writing in 2022. She can be found on Instagram @bjohnswrites

17

KITCHEN CONVERSATIONS

BY JULIE THOMASON

I am a snob. I do not like to be used for instant coffee. I'm made from delicate porcelain, a fusion of teal and jade. I have a beautiful Japanese flower blossom watercolour decorating both sides. My handle is slight, sufficient for a finger and a thumb. Forcing the drinker to take refined sips, sensing real intense coffee that sits inside of me, enhanced with the tiniest sprinkling of sugar.

The door slams, I can hear bags being dropped in the hallway. I hear him pacing towards the kitchen. He fills the kettle, opens a cupboard door and pulls out the tea bags. He's vulgar, he chucks a tea bag into the mug, pouring in water from the freshly boiled kettle. I chat with the teapot often, at how sad he feels at being used so little. There is a reason for my being, he would say after everything has been loaded into the dishwasher. Tea can infuse in me, it's more economical as you get more than one cup, from a bag in a cup, and of course the flavour, can't be compared.

Speed is of the essence; I would agree, regularly. These people don't know how to relax and appreciate life. I moaned a lot about the proliferation of instant coffee, the product of industrialisation. I shuddered to think of what happened to the beans in that process. Removing flavour and character, making everything so ubiquitous, so functional. There was no feeling, no emotion, Chuck in the coffee granules, fling over some boiling water, a glug of milk, hey presto a warm beverage.

'I admire the Japanese,' said the teapot, 'they have a ritual around tea. They respect every element, the leaves, the water, the heat, the steam, in slow gentle stages appreciating simplicity, purity. the fresh flavours and array of aromas. He's used the mug again, so we're not going to suffocate in the putrid fumes of the dishwasher as it gets crammed full of soiled items.'

'I know, everything gets placed in there, I tend not to be used because I am not dishwasher safe. My partner was destroyed that way. I like to think that's why they broke up. Clearly couldn't appreciate the finer things in life. I'm allowed to sit as decoration getting covered in the stoor from the cooking, not that a lot of that takes place.'

'I am a relic of a former partner as well; he's clearly not learned,' replied the tea pot. He was wholesome and round with an English country garden flowers decorating one side. 'It's into the microwave with most things and when more adventurous the new 'in' thing - the air fryer. It makes some horrid noises as it bleeps and whirrs.'

'They are killing themselves. Everything at full pace ahead, plugged into gadgets all the time, yet the simple pleasure of life, the healthy ones, simple cooked meals eaten at the table, conversations with friends face to face.'

'Yes, quite, not in front of the TV or a screen while eating at the same time, some reheated ready meal or a quick fix.'

As if to prove their point, he returned to the kitchen, pulled out a ready meal packet from the fridge, popped it in the microwave and made another mug of tea.

Hearing the TV being switched on, the coffee cup spat out the words, ‘he didn’t even rinse out his cup.’

The teapot sighed, there is no hope for me then, like yourself we sit and collect kitchen grime, unused or appreciated.

The coffee cup replied, ‘at least we have each other for our daily reflections on life.’

Kitchen Conversations by Julie Thomason © 2024

Julie has been composing poetry for over 30 years; her poems typically begin with a phrase or sentence that resonates with her. She explores feelings, reactions to people, places, things, and events. Julie studied English Literature at university and later taught English as a Foreign Language (EFL) in Spain. What was originally intended as a nine-month stay turned into twenty-three years of living there. Fluent in Spanish, she composes in and translates between both languages. Translating has been a fascinating and instructive process, revealing new meanings, better word choices, and nuanced perspectives through the prism of a different language. She became deeply involved in Primary English as a foreign language, which led to her first publications —textbooks in primary EFL.

Julie performs poetry at spoken word events. During the lockdown, she focused on writing and participated in Zoom writing classes, where she wrote flash fiction for the first time. Encouraged by these groups, she submitted her work and had her first poems published in 2020. In 2022, she published her first poetry collection, The Possibility of Pebbles, a set of poems inspired by the Japanese Tea Ceremony. In 2023, her first flash fiction piece, The Acrobat's Wheel, was published in the Lothlorien Poetry Journal, along with a poem titled Golden Manifestation and a series of haikus on the theme of night and day.

18

GROWING PAINS

CONTENT WARNING

BY HEATHER D HAIGH

Water pours from your nose, dragging snot with it. You can handle that. But it would kill you if you cried.

'Ready to try without the float?' Mrs Price peers down at you with one eyebrow raised.

Huge. Toilet stink//deep//deep//crackled light//high as the sky//stealing your breath your breath deep high deep.

Squealing//splashing. Soggy costume sagging like you weed yourself//peed yourself. Bleachy puddles icking your feet. Deep deep echoes echoes like the nothing in your belly. What if you sink down down where things lurk with teeth and claws that pinch and bite and squeeze squeeze away every breath every breath every breath?

You long to cling on and on, but everyone's looking watching all watching, so you'll do it. You will.

,

'So. Your last session.' The therapist flashes an encouraging smile.' Have you planned how you'll maintain progress? Have you found your safe space?'

,

School will be dry. You'll smell pencil shavings, chalk, and paper. So what if Johnny Miller nips your leg and draws pictures of you with spiders in your hair. Stupid nit-nurse. So what if he whispers Smelly Nellie. There'll be Manchester tart for lunch and maybe seconds with custard up to the rim of a clean bowl. When you get home there'll be bread and marg to be nibbled quiet as a mouse, still as a mouse, small as a mouse, and you'll pray they won't start fighting.

You'll pray harder he won't come to kiss you goodnight.

,

If you could breathe you could think if you could think you could breathe if the coils would loosen if only there was somewhere to run. Run. Run in the dark and cold with rustlings and snappings away from the streetlights along the train line. Run. The rails sing the song of the woman that woman last year that woman—did she run? did she hear this song like a siren? a siren. Run past houses and trees and trees and trees and brambles a dead pigeon and mud and trees and trees and black and grey and grey and grey and grey.

Breathe.

And grey.

Sag.

And grey.

You're glad the walk back is long. You'll be dog-tired when you get home.

You pass a woman out early, holding the hand of a small boy. 'When will I be big enough, though, Mum? When?'

'I know it feels like forever now,' she replies. 'But you'll soon look back and realise forever flew by as fast as an aeroplane.'

You go home, curl up in a ball, and whisper, 'When will I be big enough?'

,

Your first Saturday afternoon at youth club makes you want to bounce around like the balloons hanging from the paint-chipped ceiling. You dash from ping-pong, to football, to collage, to pottery, to Cluedo and Kerplunk, and all the while the mirror ball glitters the room with rainbow dots and you sing along to Crocodile Rock.

The group leader announces a change of plan. Meetings will be on Saturday mornings from next week.

You know Saturday morning is for chores; you can do what you like after lunch.

I'm not having that din under my roof. Turn it off.

You think I made a lovely bedroom for you to use it like a junk cupboard? Let's see it spick and span, and be quick about it; Mike and I need some time to ourselves.

Don't be melodramatic, your friends can't have gone far.

Amuse yourself, can't you?

,

The physio says your posture's a little better, but you've a lot of years slouching to make up for. *Hence the pain.*

,

You're sticking your chest out at my husband, again. Should have known you'd be trouble.

,

Your therapist asks why you hide burnt saucepans from your husband.

Why you write words and words and words in crimson, then scribble them out with fat scarlet marker pens, daub over the lot with clots of thick gloss paint in alizarin, carmine and madder.

Why you eat Jaffa cakes by the packet.

,

The apple pie you made in Domestic Science has charred edges and a soggy bottom.

What a waste of money. Barely edible. Ingredients are expensive you know. How much do you think I get for your keep?

You know about bloody knickers, though you're unsure about tampons and virginity, and you don't know what Foster Mother uses. No evidence in this bathroom—not here where the loo roll hides under the lace skirts of a po-faced china doll.

You cringe as you whisper, 'I think I started my periods.'

Foster Mother's lip curls while her eyebrows disappear into her starched white headband.

You burrow into the Axminster, longing to vanish like every speck of dirt, as Foster Mother impersonates you to Mrs Brown. *Making such a fuss. Silly girl.*

Mrs Brown says nothing as she slips another morsel of sour cream scone with strawberry jam between her lips.

,

You admit to your therapist you still hide chocolate wrappers in your pillowcase, where you can just catch the scent—bitter, bitter, sweet.

,

You were both sixteen. You thought it was love. He knew it was sex. You thought it was forever. He knew it was until that skinny blonde came along. You thought you'd die.

,

You were sixty-three. You thought it was a heart attack. Your doctor said it was a panic attack. You thought your number was up this time.

,

You close the laptop sharply. There's a hole in your belly, the size of a fist. You let it sit—open and hungry. You can do this.

The hole weeps a little—a thin bloody liquid.

You gather up mounds of Vinted clothes and CDs, toss them on your bed and begin to sweep the floor, cranking up the volume on your new Barbie Pink boombox—an eBay bargain. No point getting silly, now.

Thrusting the broom handle out like a mic stand, you belt out *Big Girls Don't Cry*.

Heather is a sight-impaired spoonie and emerging working-class writer from Yorkshire. Her work has been published by Fictive Dream, The Phare, Free Flash Fiction, WestWord and others. She has won competitions with New Writers and Globe Soup. Find her at: haigh19c.wixsite.com/heatherbooknook
x.com/HeatherBookNook
facebook.com/Heatherbooknook
instagram.com/heatherbooknook/
threads.net/@heatherbooknook

PART IV

'I AM CONSTANTLY TRYING TO COMMUNICATE SOMETHING INCOMMUNICABLE...

TO EXPLAIN SOMETHING INEXPLICABLE, TO TELL ABOUT SOMETHING I ONLY FEEL IN MY BONES.' NOVEMBER 1920, FRANZ KAFKA, LETTERS TO MILENA, TRANSLATED BY PHILIP BOEHM

Today, I woke up and had more fingers than I had the night before, and they were growing longer as I looked at them. They were itching, itching. But why was I itching? What did I roll around in when I was asleep? My skin must have developed a great sensitivity. Where has all my hair gone? Gone? Gone? Or had it really gone? Just a mirage? Or had it really existed at all? If so, where exactly had it gone? I felt broken and useless. I couldn't imagine what everyone must think of me was left, other than the memory of that I had lived a different life in the past. Now this had all disappeared and I felt lost... What should I do? I needed to formulate a plan.

An 'exquisite corpse' micro-fiction from Bodleian Libraries' writing workshops

19

HIS BONES

BY MADELYN POSTMAN

If his bones could speak, they would plead, *Take us home.*

'Ha!' His voice would echo off the walls of his hillside crypt in Oakland. 'Who do you take me for, an old-fashioned immigrant?' He speaks English with no accent.

You've certainly taken on American ways, here in Gold Mountain. But your soul will not be at peace until we return to China. Though it's thousands of miles away, we're still entangled with our homeland. Whatever happens over there, I simultaneously feel it here. Nobody said this was going to be easy. You're resourceful – figure it out.

'My dear bones, I worked so hard to get here. Think of the miles we walked as a boy between the villages, Long Tow Wan to Shakee, selling eggs to scrape together my fare to California. With all that trodding on stone paths, it's a miracle that you made me grow so tall.'

The bones, pleased with the recognition, indulge Joe. They chuckle. *Such a long time ago. Remember grandmother, Maa-Maa, and her sour face, like it was being sucked from the inside? She's the one who put the fire under you to leave home. She was jealous of the Gold Mountain wives and wanted to be dripping in gold jewellery like them.*

'Shame that she didn't live to see my wealth. She wouldn't have believed her eyes. I would have given her all the gold earrings and bangles she desired.' Joe sounds nostalgic.

One of the first Chinese American millionaires. You were in the New York Times – 'High Salaries Paid in Nation, 1937' – alongside Walt Disney and Charlie Chaplin. The bones keep the score, as if they could take all the credit for the transformation: founding the National Dollar Stores; selling off stock market shares a hair ahead of the 1929 crash; investing in property in California, Hawaii, Nevada.

You couldn't have done it without me. While he was alive, the bones had made Joe stand arrow-straight: proud and oddly formal.

But Joe isn't listening. 'I didn't even ask for help from the Chinese Six Companies. I don't take charity. I give it. You know, it's the Chinese Six Companies who went across America digging up emigrants' skeletons and shipping them back to China through Hong Kong and Macau. Twenty thousand pounds of bones, making the journey of their dreams in reverse.

'After that, the only bones that got shipped across the Pacific were cattle shin bones from Chicago, to be made into mahjong sets in Shanghai and sent back to America. Cheaper than ivory. But that was back in the '20s, forty years ago!'

The bones have heard it all before. They sigh, then regret it. They need to be patient – looks like they're here with Joe for all eternity.

Do you get the irony?

'What irony?' Joe is guarded.

We're stuck in Mountain View Cemetery, here in Gold Mountain.

Fifty-seven years pass.

Listen!

Joe makes out muffled voices, different to the docents who stop by the crypt marked 'SHOONG' to reel off a two-minute synopsis of his life.

A woman's voice marvels, 'I can't believe we're here in person. I saw it on YouTube.'

Another woman, older: 'Let's take a selfie!'

The younger woman asks, 'What would I have called him? Tai-Goong, great-grandfather?'

The older woman responds, 'I don't know the right name in Cantonese. I think he was my Goong-Goong? I was little when he died.'

Joe and his bones hold their breath while the two women outside shuffle around.

The older woman says, bubbly, 'One, two, three, cheese!'

A camera shutter clicks. Then everything is quiet once more.

Joe whispers, 'She said she was little... must be my son's youngest daughter. And the great-granddaughter – who is she?'

His clavicles raise in a shrug.

While the great-granddaughter was at the crypt, the bones transmitted their wishes to her. She felt it as a wave of emotion, then a sudden sense of connection to her great-grandfather. The bones became entangled with her, linking four generations.

She begins to research her ancestor tenaciously, like a dog

with a bone, as if his history could enhance her life with meaning. She notes that he was born in 1879. The date seems disembodied, so she looks up other people born that year. Albert Einstein is one. She goes on a tangent reading about the scientist and finds that he described quantum entanglement as 'spooky action at a distance.' Entanglement fascinates her. A headline about Chinese scientists working with 'six weirdly connected photons' reminds her of the Chinese Six Companies shipping emigrants' bones home so their souls would be at rest.

She feels compelled to dig in, to get closer. She travels to Zhongshan, a ferry ride away from Hong Kong, and locates Joe's house in the nearby village of Long Tow Wan. Her great-grandfather's homeland is blurry through her tears. The past and the present, China and Gold Mountain, have reunited and condensed into this one powerful moment.

,

Back in America, the great-granddaughter excavates a storage unit that houses generations of family history. She discovers three relics.

A National Dollar Stores thirtieth-year commemoration plaque listing all the store openings since 1907.

A black and white headshot of Joe mounted next to a Memorial Resolution from the Board of Directors marking their chairman's passing to 'the Great Beyond from whence no traveller returns' on April 13, 1961.

A full-length oil painting of Joe standing next to a chair, wearing a double-breasted suit, left hand tucked into his pocket.

The great-granddaughter and a weirdly-connected task force – a university librarian, an artist, a personal trainer, an import-export business owner, a museum director – arrange for the artifacts to travel by truck and then cargo ship, leaving Gold Mountain and cutting across the swells of the Pacific, all the way to China.

Thanks to the Somewhat Chinese Six People, the representations of Joe and his life's work now live a two-hour walk from his ancestral home, in the Zhongshan Museum.

,

His bones sigh, relieved, *I knew you could do it.*

Madelyn Postman is writing a short story collection that links memoir with her family's intergenerational tale of Chinese and Eastern European Jewish immigrants to California. The first story in the collection, 'Things My Dad Told Me,' will be published in The Hope Prize anthology by Simon & Schuster Australia in December 2024. Her stories have been longlisted in Flash 500 Short Stories 2024 and her work has been featured on The Failing Writers' Podcast. She is American and lives outside London with her husband and two teenage children. You can find her on Instagram @the16stories.

20

CHOOSE YOUR ANIMAL

BY SARA HILLS

And when it's my turn to reframe the past, I say they were javelinas. I say it was winter and describe the snow flaking onto pear-shaped cactus pads, a crystalline white overlaid on the blue-gray and green. I say what we've all heard before: javelinas are mostly harmless but they get hungry, restless, like the rest of us.

Around the circle, plastic chairs creak under the weight of nodding faces. Each one its own collision of particles, arranged and rearranged into unique fractals that understand the complexities of pain.

I say it was late afternoon. Red sun sluicing the horizon. Javelinas clicking their canines with a shivering sound, swigging beer warm as blood. How the javelinas taught me to pray.

How, years later, a guitar riff or a whiff of crushed pine would drop me back into that basement wallow of an Eastside apartment complex: javelinas pounding their hooves on the tiles, punching through TV channels and finding God wearing the face of George Burns and that dead singer, John Denver, pleading *why me*, asking *does God really exist?* But I don't ask the circle if they remember the movie

Oh, God! or that George Burns lived to a hundred or if any of them still believe in miracles.

And no one reminds me that javelinas are matriarchal animals. In this circle, we don't dispute the speaker. We know even Jeffrey Epstein had a mother and once heeded her call. We know the mind goes places that the body can't follow.

Supplanting our memories with animals is supposed to allow us distance; distance is supposed to allay our shame. For Marta, it was a grizzly. For Gretchen, a golden retriever. For me, I stare at the round faces of my knees. I hug the comfort pillow closer, fold my body into a tight knot, imagining each curled knob of my spine sprouting wings.

Did you know you can feel a javelina's ribs through its coat?

I don't know why I say that. Immediately, I want to take it all back. I want to reframe my past with a different animal, a mouse. A flea. Something I can stab out with my smallest finger.

But erasure has never worked. So now, I'm supposed to make it real. Mundane. To say the javelinas rooted in the trash. To talk about the commotion, the musk-heavy snuffling, their twig-thin legs and flared brutal faces. To say a javelina's lifespan is short short short. How they only weigh forty, maybe fifty pounds. A bag of potatoes. A sack of dirt.

Who wakes in the night afraid of a sack of dirt?

Marta whispers that she was no more than a berry—*sometimes girls are just plucked small*—but it's been forty years. When will she be able to grow into something else?

Each face around the circle echoes her question, echoes and mirrors my winter tale back to me. How we were sprinting, laughing. How the snow fell weightless. The sideways angle of January light.

My foot vibrates. I was fourteen. Slick-skinned. Skinny.

Javelinas have scent glands beneath their eyes and near the base of their tails and thirty-eight teeth. Tusks sharp as razors.

In the movie, God appears in the unlikeliest places: in the supermarket, in the car radio, in the bathroom when John Denver is showering, alone and naked, his round glasses perched on the cluttered countertop next to his razor.

God tells him to shave.

The walls of the community center are faded blue and the floor is formed of cheap gray vinyl, squares peeled and stuck, peeled and glued into place. Gridlines of rows and columns. Someone, on hands and knees, had to lay each one, each ugly square of this fake stone tile. After laying the first one, did they realize it would take forever? Did they look out over the room and imagine no end in sight?

None of us move from the circle. Not to use the restroom or make a quick call. Not to drink the drip black coffee which reeks of the past.

The circle affords me all the patience I don't allow myself. Like when Gretchen says golden retrievers are supposed to be gentle. Loyal. Protectors of children. We let the words hang themselves on the silence. No one coughs. No one cries. We are a collective desert; we have already given.

Did you know a herd of javelinas is called a squadron?

The inevitability of what happened next on that winter afternoon is not what the circle is about. We know first-hand the ferocity of animal behavior. We know the body goes places that the mind can't allow itself to follow.

Instead, the circle waits for me to finish, for the memory to evaporate from my bones, like waking from a haunting to find gold light filtering in from a high window, dappling lace-like patterns across the worn tile floor.

Choose Your Animal by Sara Hills © 2024

Sara Hills is the author of the award-winning flash collection The Evolution of Birds. Her work has been widely published in anthologies and magazines, including The Best Small Fictions, SmokeLong Quarterly, Bath Flash Fiction Award, Fractured Lit, and elsewhere. You can find her online @sarahillswrites.

21

THE GLORY

CONTENT WARNING

BY MAEVE CONLON

Some men can sense death in the air the same way they can sense coming rain. The scent is heavy, the air is hot and dense, waiting for that final moment of release before the cleansing can begin. In the mountains of the Sierra Maestra, there was no shortage of rain or death, and Cedro had a nose for both.

Gloria al Padre...

The dye from the rosary around his neck had stained his skin a sickly blue. A fellow soldier had bought it for him in Havana during one of their last supply runs. The plastic mold felt cheap, nothing like the heavy wooden beads from his childhood. He kissed the hot plastic crucifix every morning before patrol and counted the decades every night to go to sleep. He knew others in the camp judged these traditions– saw no place for them in the new order. But for Cedro, who was raised with nothing, his faith was his only true possession in the world.

Jimeno had asked for a rosary too, but his request was ignored. He had asked to use Cedro's in the meantime, but his nagging was in vain. Although the cousins had shared everything as children, war had quickly taught Cedro that any affection between them now was fodder for the other soldiers to use in their mocking. Cedro had endured these insults since they were boys, when he had stood his ground proudly in defense of his cousin. But now, as men, Cedro felt the burden of Jimeno's incompetence boiling a black resentment in his stomach. And as the bile rose in the throat, so his growing irritation searched for a release.

Y al Hijo...

The sick tent was a furnace in the late afternoon sun. Men cooked beneath the tarp, their bare skin covered in sheets of sweat. Jimeno lay on his side with his knees pulled up to his chin. Cedro watched his cousin's concave stomach shudder with the hunger of each breath. As the body faded, the lungs always became greedier. The smell of sweat and linen beckoned a memory to the surface and Cedro was suddenly reminded of when they'd shared a bed as children. The strict masculinity of the daytime was absolved upon the straw mattress and affection aroused laughter, touch, and talk of dreams yet to come. Talk of a future disinherited by the dirt-stained nails of their forefathers. A new beginning of something greater. Something glorious.

'I'm going to be a soldier one day.'

'What will I do, Cedro?'

'You can be a soldier too.'

'I don't want to – I'm not strong like you.'

'Don't worry Jimeno, I'll take care of you!'

But now, as Cedro looked at his dying cousin, he felt nothing but impatience.

Y al Espíritu Santo...

Jimeno's eyes stirred beneath the closed lids, but they didn't open until Cedro raised the cool coffee to his nose. Jimeno sat up weakly and accepted the gift. With the last gulp, Jimeno's eyes fell enviously on the plastic rosary.

'They still haven't gotten mine.'

Cedro pulled the beads over his head without a word and offered them. Jimeno looked cautious, a kicked dog wary of acts of kindness. Cedro shook the beads once, a warning that the offer might be rescinded, and Jimeno snatched it hungrily. Too weak to lift his arms, Jimeno maneuvered his head awkwardly into the necklace's opening. Once it was on, he met his cousin's gaze proudly, his boyish face bright with self-satisfaction. Cedro swallowed the lump in his throat, a stone dropping into his empty stomach so loud he feared Jimeno would hear the echo.

'C'mon, it's our turn to fetch water. You need to stretch your legs.'

Como era en el principio...

Last night's campfire fire had felt stiflingly hot, but Cedro was excited that the Commander had asked for his company.

'He's become an albatross around your neck, hm?'

The Commander's voice was heavy with cigar smoke and sleep. Cedro was silent, he just watched the reflection of the flames dapple the butt of his rifle. Before the war, Cedro had never fired a gun. But like so many of his childhood comrades, the war had forced Cedro to become a soldier before he had had time to become a man. When he was first recruited, the metal felt awkward in his calloused hands. Hands that had been bred for tilling the soft mountain dirt. Hands that were taught to nurture life from the earth, not bury men beneath it.

But it will all be worth it. Cedro recited this plea to himself as faithfully as his nightly prayers. *It will be worth it. It will be glorious... it has to be.*

The Commander rested the cigar between his polished fingers.

'Tell me, comrade, have you ever heard the saying, "The greater the sacrifice, the greater the glory"?'

Ahora y siempre...

The clouds hung close to the trees, creating an artificial skyline, trapping the oppressive humidity beneath. Cedro turned his neck up to the sky, sniffing the air.

'The rain will come any minute.'

By the time they reached the river, Jimeno's laboured breathing was nearly deafening. He stumbled over to a moss-covered boulder and sprawled his thin body on the cushioning. He watched his cousin fill the buckets without offering any help, and knowing Cedro would not ask for it.

'How long is this gonna take?'

Cedro kept his mouth shut for fear that if he opened it, he might give himself away with the putridity on his breath, that black bile of resentment that had finally bubbled to the surface.

'Cedro?'

Por los siglos, de los siglos...

When it was all over, Cedro washed in the river. Submersing himself until he could feel the soft mud below. The cool water felt good against his tear-stung cheeks. He rubbed the water into his eyes, sucked it into his mouth, raked it through his hair, and by the time he ascended to the surface, the rain had finally come.

Amen.

Maeve Conlon is a 26-year-old Irish-Canadian writer from Windsor, Ontario. She graduated from the University of Windsor with a bachelor's in History and a minor in English Literature and is currently working as a librarian. . She has had short stories published by both Elegant Literature Magazine and The Quagmire Literary Journal and continues to write as much as possible between (and sometimes at) work.

22

THE LIFE CYCLE OF FROGS

NEW VOICE PRIZE

BY VICTORIA HARRIS

5. Tadpoles

There they are: translucent blobs and tails like commas wriggling and squirming in the tank. Little mouth parts mowing away at the algae. Andie's face is pressed up against the tank, big green eyes growing wide like forest pools as she watches. It's the first time her parents have brought her to see my lab. They're exhausted from the long flight but Andie just couldn't wait.

Andie's face twists in disgust. 'Eew!' she says.

No granddaughter of mine is going to be repulsed by tadpoles.

'They're not eew,' I say, 'Frogs are beautiful. A gardener's best friend: they eat up all the slugs that destroy my vegetables.'

'Why are there so many of them?' she asks.

I settle myself down in a chair next to the sequencing machine and beckon Andie over. 'It's a hard life being a tadpole. Most of them would usually get eaten up. In the wild maybe one or two will ever get to be a frog. These ones are special: they're endangered. You know what endangered means?'

Andie shakes her head.

'It means that there's not many left in the wild. Humans pollute or destroy their habitats or they die from parasites. That's why we look after them here and try to make sure as many survive as possible.'

I frown as I notice the slight murkiness: I've told them before we need better filters.

18. Froglets

The summer weather is close and the froglets are starting to leave the pond. As Andie clutches that envelope apprehensively, I can still see that little girl, staring at the water with me.

'Are you going to open that?' I ask.

Her hands are shaking as she tears it open slowly and pulls out the letter. The tears start to well as she reads the words on the Cambridge letterheaded paper. I can tell without even looking at it what the outcome must be.

9. Hindlegs

It's late spring and the tadpoles have the first signs of back legs emerging. Andie and I are sitting by the pond in the garden of my little country cottage. It's nice to be back closer to my family, somewhere that's not a long-haul flight away. A dragonfly larva has a tadpole in its clutches, which is writhing and squirming to break free but I can already tell its hopeless.

'Aren't you going to help it?' Andie asks.

'Nothing to be done,' I reply.

The dragonfly nymph sucks out the tadpole's insides

and Andie's eyes start to well up. One more tadpole that will never be a frog.

'That's nature, I'm afraid. Like I told you before, most of those will never become frogs, but the dragonfly needs to live too.' I say.

54. Adulthood

It's autumn now and the frogs will have already left the pond. The images from the ceremony on the screen dance in front of my eyes. My eyes are going, so I have to squint. The nurses have brought be extra pillows to prop me up, so I can see Andie on the screen and behind her a picture of my old friend.

'Thank you all,' screen Andie says. 'I want first of all to thank my grandmother for instilling in me the passion for research. This specimen was bred in my grandmother's lab where its genome was sequenced. Without that basis, I would never have been able to make the connection between these genetics and their application to human diseases.'

18. Froglets

It's been two weeks and the froglets are starting to lose their tails. The ones that made it will be leaving soon. Andie turns another letter over in her hands.

'I know it's not Cambridge,' I say, 'But it's an excellent university.'

Come late November, I'm on a train with Andie's favourite chocolate cake for her birthday.

I arrive at her dorm, and as I gently knock, Andie opens the door. I can tell straight away that something is wrong. I sit down next to her on the bed, which is the only place in this small room.

'Jen and I had a fight,' she says, looking at her feet.

'Your girlfriend Jen, right?'

Andie's eyes go wide.

'Just because I'm old doesn't mean I'm not perceptive. No-one cries like that over just a good friend.'

She clutches her hands, refusing to meet my eyes.

'She dumped me,' she says.

'You know what they say,' I say. 'You have to kiss a lot of frogs before you find your princess.'

She wipes her eyes and lets out a small laugh.

'I thought you liked frogs, and you always said they were beautiful?' she says.

'You're right,' I concede, 'Well, how about this? There'll be a lot of tadpoles in your life but only some of them will get to be frogs. Don't worry, someday you'll find the frog that will be your princess.'

29. Losing tails

Andie looks stunning.

'Here,' I say, pinning the frog brooch to her dress. 'Something old.'

'Your favourite brooch. Thank you,' she says.

'It's your brooch, now. Better not be late,' I say. 'Don't want to leave Sophie waiting.'

5. Frog

My heart sinks as I take it in. The fungus has contaminated almost all the tanks. I told them the filters were not good enough. And yet, I know in my heart that this is my responsibility. How could I have messed up so badly?

We sterilise and treat everything, but I already know in my heart that for most of them it is too late. Only a handful of tadpoles make it. As the weeks pass, we lose more, until by the end of the season only one remains. Out of a clutch of 500, only one has actually gotten to be a frog. Maybe that will be enough.

Victoria is an Oxfordshire-based researcher with an interest in speculative fiction and science. They are particularly intrigued by the interplay between science and philosophy.

PART V

'WE SUDDENLY TURN OURSELVES ENTIRELY IN THE OPPOSITE DIRECTION, LIKE A WEATHER VANE IN THE MOUNTAINS.'

THE DIARIES OF FRANZ KAFKA 1910-1913, TRANSLATED BY JOSEPH KRESH

Today, I woke up and let out a cry as I looked in the mirror. My chestnut curls had turned grey, and my hair was straight and straggly. My face was distorted like one of those mirrors you see at the fair. The hair was too long, one eye too dark. I was afraid of my reflections and so I ran out of my house and into the street, and all the people bustling about were wrong somehow too. Their movements were odd. I couldn't quite put my finger on it. They looked strange. Staccato, jerky movements – inhuman somehow. And yet I recognised them from somewhere. Within a dark recess of my mind, a memory was trying to emerge, and I opened my mind to the possibilities.

An 'exquisite corpse' micro-fiction from Bodleian Libraries' writing workshops

23

WHAT STORMS MAY COME

BY P. A BEAUDOIN

They gave *me* the stupid rabbit costume.

When I balked, Robert, the Grand High Thinks He's So Great Just Cuz His Uncle Owns This Pathetic Excuse For A Theme Park said, 'For cryin' out loud, Teddy! All the kids love Bouncy Bunny. You'll be a big hit. Now, get dressed and get out.'

The costumes were hung in the staff lunch room, which doubled as our change room. The head pieces were suspended on hooks with the body costumes on wire hangers underneath. As soon as I got the headpiece in place, I knew ole Bouncy's frenzied eyes had not seen the inside of a washing machine in a very long time. I started to say something about it until Robert clamped his hand over Bouncy's wide open, fanatically grinning mouth, and everything went dark, as that was the only space I could look through.

'You *never* speak when you're in costume! *Never*! And you

never appear in public without your costume. Do you understand?'

I nodded my bulbous head.

He as much as pushed me out the door. 'And don't forget the dance!' he yelled after me.

Oh yeah.

There's a dance.

There's always a dance.

The things I did for minimum wage.

I saw her as soon as my eyes adjusted to the bright sunlight. She was sitting on a bench, away from the noise and Saturday afternoon pedestrian traffic, bent forward, her face buried in her hand, obviously crying.

'Ah!' I whispered to myself. 'My first Moper.'

That's what we called them. Mopers. People in emotional distress, giving off all kinds of bad energy. And we can't have bad energy in the park now, can we. Upon encountering a Moper, the character performers, like me, were obliged to engage with them and do everything in our power to cheer them up. You've probably guessed by now, this is where 'the dance' comes in. If we failed to illicit the requisite level of cheerfulness, we would gently escort them to our wise and compassionate security guards who would in turn gently escort them out of the park.

And then all would be as it should be, with everyone happy, happy, happy.

The lower part of Bouncy's costume, his haunches I guess you'd say, were clearly intended for a man more portly than myself, and I had to keep pulling them up to keep from tripping. I gathered up both sides as well as I could in my thickly padded paw-gloves and proceeded to dance over to my damsel in distress.

'Dance' is *so* not the right word.

Lurch. I lurched over to her and did what might have passed for a dance had it not been for the size 23 bunny slippers and the haunches periodically settling around my ankles. After a few steps to the left and a few to the right and a pirouette here and a jete' there, I realized my damsel was not looking at me. She hadn't even raised her head. My oafish feet slowed, then stopped, embarrassed. Her grief was so evident, I felt like I was dancing at a funeral.

I watched her for a bit, then, don't ask me why, I sat down next to her. It felt OK. Like she didn't mind. I just looked around and knocked my bunny slippers together now and then to pass the time.

After a while, still not looking at me, she reached over and took my paw. And somehow, I knew just what to do. I pulled off my other paw-glove between my knees, and gently placed my hand over hers. And we sat there, together, and I was so unspeakably happy, I wanted to cry.

I don't know how long we sat there like that, but she startled me when, looking straight ahead, she asked quietly, 'What's your name?'

'Teddy,' I said. 'Uh, Theodore actually.'

She nodded. 'Thank you, Theodore.'

My response fell so short of her graciousness.

'Sure,' I said.

She squeezed my hand and stood up, squared her shoulders against what storms may come, and walked away into the crowd.

I watched her until she disappeared, and only then became aware of my fingers pulling off my other paw-glove. Then both hands went to work unlatching my headpiece.

I decided not to interfere with their work.

And then oh! the air! The *air*! So fresh and cool and lovely and pure! I breathed it in and felt reborn.

I stood up, threw the paw-gloves into the headpiece, situated said headpiece under my arm, and slogged back toward the staff room.

On the way, I created something of a stir.

Children, lacking the vocabulary to express their horror at Bouncy's astonishing transformation, let projectile vomiting do the talking for them. Mothers screamed, and fathers, well, fathers took pictures.

I pushed open the Employees' Only door and staggered inside.

It was lunch hour and the room was thrumming with the laughter and conversation of the other performers. It took them a couple moments to notice me, and when they did, a shocked silence took possession of the room. They had never seen a performer enter through that door out of costume, out of character, clearly out of his mind.

All chewing ceased.

A few of them stood up, maybe in awe, or maybe in some kind of tribute. I shuffled to an empty table, fished the paw-gloves out of the headpiece, and positioned it just so. I brushed off the dust, and adjusted the floppy ears.

Then I pummelled the ever-living crap out of it!

When finished, I placed the headpiece back on its hook, floppy ears now dangling under its chin, then shucked the rest of the costume, slid it onto the hanger and carefully set it underneath.

My work done, I turned around, squared my shoulders against what storms may come, and walked out.

It was the opinion of all those gathered there that day, that Bouncy Bunny never looked better.

Penny-Anne Beaudoin earned a Master's Degree in Pastoral Ministry in 1997 and has published articles pertaining to religion and spirituality in several Canadian and American journals. She was nominated for the Canadian Church Press Award in 2000. Her fiction has been published in Lorraine and James, Writers On Line, Ascent Aspirations, Flash Me, FreeFall Magazine, The Rose & Thorn, Skive Magazine, The Canadian Writers' Journal, and flashquake. She was nominated for the Push Cart Prize in 2005, and won the gold medal in the Wenlock Olympian Society Short Story Competition in 2022. 'holy cards: dead women talking', (Black Moss Press), is her collection of first-person poems about women saints, and was published in 2009.

24

THE WORST-CASE SCENARIO

SECOND PLACE PRIZE WINNER

BY EMILY RINKEMA

At the end of the first week at my new job, Tina from Sales makes me go to a lunchtime baby shower with her. I can't think of many things that could be worse–maybe a pap smear, maybe a water park, maybe a plane crash–but she tells me I have to go, that it'll make a good impression.

There are about twenty women in the conference room, which is decorated with blue streamers and blue balloons. Some are seated already, a semi-circle with the mom-to-be in a rocking chair at the front, but most are at the potluck table.

We get in line behind Carla from Communications, who is filling her plate with desserts.

'She's just glowing,' Tina says to me, looking at the expectant mother, who I think works in Finance. 'I just love babies,' she says, and I scoop something from the bowl in front of me onto my plate. The table is covered in all things boy: trucks, trains, cars, baseballs, airplanes. 'Look how happy she is,' she says, and tucks her chin to her shoulder like she's cuddling herself.

I'm not sure she's glowing, but she does seem happy to be having a baby.

We only have 30 minutes for lunch, so a woman with curly hair who I think works in Marketing tells us all to have a seat and says we're going to play a game called Funny Story. She goes over the rules: the mom-to-be will pull a name out of a bonnet, and the person whose name is pulled has to tell a quick funny story about being a mom, or, she says, if she isn't a mother, then she should tell a funny story about her own mother, or, she says, laughing, if she isn't a mother and doesn't have a mother, then she can tell any funny story that has a mother in it. At the end, the mother-to-be will choose the funniest story.

I'm relieved no one knows me yet, that my name won't have made it into the bonnet because I never RSVP'd. I'm probably the only one in the room who is not a mother, who doesn't have a mother, who doesn't want to be a mother, who is the Marketing woman's worst-case scenario. I start to eat.

But the pregnant one, the one with the t-shirt that says BABY with an arrow pointing down, says my name. I look up, mouth full of broccoli salad. Everyone is staring at me. Tina winks.

I've never been good with people. I work in IT. But Tina smiles at me expectantly and I panic and start talking, telling the first story about mothers I can think of. I tell the room that when I was ten, my mother, who would die in childbirth a few years later, told me her family always knew when my grandmother was pregnant again because they would find her sitting at the top of the stairs, crying.

The Marketing woman puts her hand to her mouth.

I remember that it's supposed to be a funny story, so I quickly clarify that she cried because she had fifteen children. 'Fifteen,' I repeat with a laugh. Everyone has stopped eating and I just keep going because they are all staring at me and there's more to the story, so I tell them that after the 15th baby was born, before she was even crawling, they were honored for being good Catholics and flew to meet the Pope, and on the way back, just hours after being blessed, their plane crashed and everyone died. 'Not the baby,' I add quickly, because this is a baby shower, and I don't want them to think I would tell a story where a baby died. 'Just the parents. All fifteen kids stayed home,' I say, and I realize that I should have said that part earlier.

Tina looks at her plate.

'Here's the funny part,' I say, because that's the point of the game, and though I may not be an extravert, I have seven siblings and equate competition with survival. As the timer goes off, I tell them, speaking quickly now so I don't get disqualified, that nine of the fifteen kids became priests and nuns. I'm laughing now, because, come on, that's funny, right? Not funny haha, but funny unexpected, funny fucking absurd.

The pregnant mother puts her right hand on her belly. She might be crying, but I look away before I can tell for sure.

The real funny thing, the thing I don't say because my time is up, is that the baby, the 15th one, the one who wasn't yet crawling when her parents crashed into the ocean, told me once–as we sat together at the top of the stairs on the morning of my tenth birthday–that she wished her mother had said, 'Not without the baby,' when she was invited to meet the Pope. Then she would have been just a beautiful photograph on the wall, a memory of a baby that, if not for tragedy, could have grown up to be anything, maybe a writer, maybe a doctor, maybe the owner of a bakery that made only pies. But instead, she told me, and she laughed, even though she was crying, she grew up to be a mother.

Emily Rinkema lives and writes in northern Vermont, USA. Her writing has appeared in The Sun Magazine, SmokeLong Quarterly, and X-R-A-Y Lit, and she has stories in the Best American Nonrequired Reading, Bath Flash, and Oxford Flash anthologies. You can read her work on her website (emilyrinkema.wixsite.com/my-site) or follow her on X or IG (@emilyrinkema).

25

SHE WRITES HERSELF A DIFFERENT LIFE

OXFORD PRIZE WINNER

BY SUSAN WIGMORE

One in which her mother doesn't die tragically giving birth even though it means sacrificing any likeness to Mary Shelley. One in which her father spends weekends at home (like other dads) instead of showing people Grand-Design houses he wants himself. One in which her older brother isn't in his room all day listening to *Dark Side of the Moon* but takes her cycling on the bike she's cleaning now, upturned on the drive, just as a red car motors up the cul-de-sac towards her house, the one right at the end with the navy front door as if the road leads here and only here and the car has come for her.

It stops. Engine idling. Time tick, ticking over.

And her narrative trajectory goes into freefall, spiralling wordlessly —

until grabbed by a
gravitational pull so strong she's like a moon compelled to
orbit an unknown planet.

Because this is where she gets in the car.

Because yes, she would like to go for a spin and the driver looks so hauntingly familiar, like a wayward maiden aunt she didn't know she had, with a snake tail necklace, fringing on her jacket and two Diet Cokes up front. (Though they need something stronger, the woman says, now she's old enough, if not quite legally, to make the world spin.)

If the girl had vocabulary enough, she'd say planetary gears in the car's transmission keep it moving optimally, but the best she can manage is it floats. So they float to the Spar on the edge of town where the woman hands her a Take That tote; she'll need it, though she won't be shopping exactly. And while the woman talks rum with the shopkeeper, the girl takes chicken sandwiches and crisps and fat black grapes, mindless of a business owner's need to balance the books.

They picnic by the reservoir in long, summer-scented grass beyond a danger sign. Arctic terns swoop over the water. Just passing through, says the woman with tanned feet so effortlessly bare. There's Bacardi and Coke in paper cups and the lurch of the world. Splashes of sunshine through trees bright as revelations.

And there's the time it takes the girl to unbuckle her sandals.

Because here is where she realises something of Mary Shelley might yet linger in the narrative of her life. So she swims, naked, slick-skinned, rising through rings on the water's surface to take oxygen from the air, warmed by rum and the thrill of drinking it despite knowing, for now at least, the road leads home.

Other than the angle of the sun, nothing has changed in the cul-de-sac when the red car pulls up at the kerb. The bike is how she left it and she spins its front wheel like a game of chance at the fair, letting it whir to a stop before tossing her sandals in the bin. She knows without seeing the woman is watching, knows without hearing the car is floating away. And she walks back into her old life, the one in which no one has noticed her absence, bare feet on cool grass, cotton dress awry, the touch of a hand still warm on her arm.

She writes herself a different life by Susan Wigmore © 2024

Susan's writing has been published, placed or listed by Reflex Fiction, Oxford Flash Fiction, the Fish Short Story Prize, Mslexia, Retreat West, the Cambridge Flash Fiction Prize and The Daily Telegraph Short Story Competition. She won inclusion in the first Fractured Lit Anthology, the Fish Flash Prize 2023 and the Globe Soup Short Memoir 2022. A flash non-fiction piece was shortlisted for the 2022 QuietManDave Prize. Her novella-in-flash was long-listed for the Bath Award 2024.

26

THREE CORNERED HAT

BY SHOSHANA LAVAN

My hat has three corners.

We are surrounded by people engulfing the road, one videoing from one corner, one from another, and one from the third.

'Take off your hat.' The head of police says. Not yet screaming.

If it didn't have three corners, it wouldn't be my hat.

'Remove your hat!' He says. He is talking louder.

My hat has three corners.

'Give me your hat!' His voice hits a hysterical note.

If it didn't have three corners, it wouldn't be my hat.

'If you don't give it to me, I will take it!' Now, he is screaming. Now he is right in my face. Now he moves as though to attack me, and grabs my hat, and strides away.

Can you see the three corners of my hat?

We see the Hamas hat. The student is sitting with me in one of the teachers' meeting rooms, talking to me, instead of with me, though she asked for a discussion. *We see the Hamas flag covering slaughtered babies, proudly covering scorched babies, triumphantly exhibiting murdered women and children. Your Hamas hat is covered in dead babies' blood.*

If my hat didn't have three corners, it wouldn't be my hat.

The students hang the Israeli flag around the school, in all its corners. I walk down the steps to the main building and there it is hanging in all its glory. Another side of my hat.

But my hat has three corners.

Why did you wear a hat with a Hamas... sorry, Palestinian flag on one side, an Israeli one on the other? Are you on the side of the Palestinians?

Yes. I am. Yes. Yes, I am. I am on their side too. I can be on both sides. In two corners.

That makes for a new corner. My hat has three corners.

Peace? You talk of peace after the 7th October?

We talk only of war! Together we will win! Together, us, together, the Jewish people! We will win!!

I bow my head so as not to let them hear me: We have already lost. The hostages. The raped women. The burning babies. We have already lost.

Now is time only to find a way to breathe after the fire and the smoke has blistered our hearts.

My hat has three corners.

One: Palestine.

Two: Israel.

Three: PalestineIsrael. IsraelPalestine.

Look. It's a peace hat. Do you hear?

DO YOU HEAR?

I wore my peace hat! My three-cornered hat.

What corner am I in? What do you mean, what corner am I in? Do I have to be in one corner? But my hat has three corners! Can't I hang out in my hat?

The police don't think so.

'Take off your hat!'

'I don't understand why I should take it off.'

'Will you take off your hat?'

'No, I won't. I won't take off my hat. Tell me why I should.'

'Take off your hat!!!'

'It's my hat. There is no law to say I have to remove my hat.'

He takes my hat. Seizes it from me.

My partner puts the head of police firmly in his own corner. Then he brings back my hat.

I do not carry on wearing it.

And now, heading home, I have no idea how soon the whole of the land will choose which corner to put me in, me and my hat.

I have no idea the videos will go to all the corners of the earth.

And with a heart full of disbelief at this new reality, I will have to fight my corner.

Shoshana Lavan is a Jewish writer, teacher, and peace-builder. Her work has appeared in various books, magazines, and online platforms. Her website is: shoshana03.wixsite.com/website

27

IN BED WITH TESLA

BY DEBRA WATERS

The night my virus peaked, Nikola Tesla sat on my bed unaware that he was dead.

I wasn't surprised to see him. I was too sick to write, so I spent my days reading books about historical figures. Of all the inventors and doctors and artists and poets, I was drawn to him most. I watched, curious, as he crossed and uncrossed his slender legs. A buzz emanated from his body and when he cracked his thumbs, bright electric sparks shot from the joints.

'Why are you here?' I asked. It was a struggle to muster pleasantries at 3am. 'To help?'

'An inventor's endeavor is essentially lifesaving,' he replied. 'And I am interested in any problem that requires a solution.' His voice was soft and vaguely European, but with a New York twang.

'Did you expect me to speak like Dracula, dear?'

'Can you read my thoughts? But you don't believe in telepathy!'

'I don't, yet it believes in me,' he said. Tesla sighed, stretched his long arms then folded his limbs like an origami master. In the low light, I saw the sharp cut of his tweed suit, his heavy brow and strong nose.

Well, this was awkward. I couldn't ask about his induction motor or electrical system (neither of which I understood) so I did what I do at parties; turned to pop culture. 'Who played you better in the films – David Bowie or Nicholas Hoult?'

'Hoult is the English actor, yes?' I nodded. 'He has my height but overcooked my accent. I shall go with Bowie.' He pronounced Bowie correctly, which impressed me.

'Why Bowie?'

'He was a master of invention, like I,' he said, matter-of-factly.

I sat up to correct my crumpled pyjamas. I didn't want this fastidious man to think of me as slovenly *and* a Luddite.

'You enjoy slumber,' he said. It was not so much a question as a criticism.

'My father used to say I reminded him of a dormouse. Do you know, the name comes from the Latin "dormire", which means "to sleep".' I was quite pleased I'd remembered this.

'Why would you wish to be compared to a rodent that wastes most of its life insensate,' he replied. 'Surely you have better aspirations for yourself.'

I bristled. 'How did you function on so little? It's not a badge of honour to be exhausted, you know.'

'I slumber. I take four hours, sometimes five.'

'But you're famous for it.'

Tesla flicked at a stray thread on his arm and a spark flashed.

'Such are the stories that maketh a man.'

I wasn't sure what to make of this but presumed that, like most successful men, he was prone to self-mythologizing. My body felt clammy and it hurt to inhale. I wanted to undress but prudery stopped me (absurd considering he was a ghost).

Lucia padded into the room, sauntered over to the dead man and rubbed her scent on his tailored suit. She showed no fear. So animals don't act as an early warning system for the supernatural after all, I thought, disappointed. I waited for Tesla to dismiss her with an electrified jab of his foot but his shiny leather boot remained perfectly still.

'I didn't take you for a cat lover,' I said.

'Cats have reinvented themselves through history. They have vision and know how to adapt to new environments. I have nothing but respect for them.'

Lucia jumped onto the inventor's lap and purred.

'Your clothes!'

'No matter.'

'But...'

'What?'

'Cats kill birds. You loved birds.'

'One never killed my birds.'

This seemed shortsighted coming from a humanist whose reason for existence was inexorably bound to humanity, who once said "we are held together, like the stars in the firmament, with ties inseparable."

'You can't pick and choose like that,' I said.

'Your mother would have saved you from a fire before a stranger's child, would she not.'

'I guess,' I replied petulantly.

'I rest my case.'

'Mr Tesla, are you here to impart knowledge that could change the world?' I said.

'Because I'm so sick my hair hurts.'

'The world has already changed. It changed as we were speaking.'

'Why are you here then? To tell me I'm dying?'

'Ah, if anything, dear, I am here to say you are not living.' Tesla tapped the side of his large, coiffured skull and bluish streams of electric shot between his head and hand. 'You do not utilise what is in here. Are you indolent? Or afraid of its power?'

'Both.'

'A lazy answer!'

'I'm afraid of what I imagine.'

'What you imagine? Or what you imagine will come to pass?

'What if my stories harm?' I winced – a migraine was blooming in my head.

'True. Art can be as persuasive as science, though Edison would have balked at the thought.' He shook his head. 'Pah! That man,' he muttered. 'What you fear is every creator's fear, but you are doing yourself a disservice if you do not put into being what your unconscious wishes to make conscious. Construct what your mind's eye has shown you.'

'So, you're here to tell me to keep writing? I'm not dying?'

'You are dying. Everyone is dying! But you are not dead yet.'

Tesla hovered his hand over Lucia and we watched her black fur rise to meet his palm. He stood, and I saw the prodigious height of the man. He brushed his suit with graceful irradiated flicks and tiny waterfalls fell to the floor.

'You will write?'

'I'll try.'

'Do not try. Do.'

I promised and held out my hand.

'I will not shake hands,' he said. 'There is too much illness in the world.'

'Why would that matter if you're dead?'

'Dead?' Tesla snorted.

'Since 1943.'

After looking unsteady for a moment, Tesla's eyes widened. 'Of course! Energy, frequency, vibration. These things really are the answer to all things!' Then, before I could respond, he bowed, recommended a cool bath for my fever, and disappeared.

In Bed with Tesla by Debra Waters © 2024

Debra lives in Brighton and writes short stories, auto-fiction, and flash fiction. In 2020, she won The Bridport Short Story Prize. She has been shortlisted for the Bath Short Story Award, Bridport Flash Fiction Prize, Pat Kavanagh Award, and London Independent Story Prize (flash).

Debra has also been longlisted for the Manchester Fiction Prize and the London Library's Emerging Writers Programme, and received a highly commended mention for the Writers & Artists Working Class Writers Prize. Her work has been published in Litro, the Bridport Prize Anthology 2020, the Bath Flash Fiction V.5 Anthology, Flash Flood, and thi wurd's 2024 Earthly Rewards anthology.

x.com/DebAshWat

28

NEBULATED

BY PETER HANKINS

Unexpectedly, a man sat down beside me.

In Airey Park there is a rise with a bench on top where you can get a really good panoramic view of the village. I was not looking at the church spire, though, nor the lovely blossoms that were surely about to fall from the old cherry trees. Instead, I was gazing at the clouds, immense white cumulus, drifting across a shining azure sky.

'I wouldn't do that,' he said. I lowered my eyes.

He was quite smartly dressed, with a tie that had been neatly tied and then roughly pulled loose. His blazer was pressed, his brogues were polished, but he was haggard and unshaven and somehow looked neglected.

'Sorry?' I said.

'Don't stare at the clouds. It's dangerous.'

'You mean it's bad for my eyes?'

He shook his head. 'Worse than that. Why do you do it? They are good at seducing the gaze of the innocent, I know. I suppose you see things in them? Castles, monsters, people?'

'No, not really. I know people talk about clouds shaped like teapots or violins. I've never seen that. I suppose I don't have that kind of imagination. To me they just look like colossal banks of water vapour. In its way, I think that's more impressive than them being a sort of celestial cartoon gallery. If there was only one place you could see the clouds, I'm sure people would travel from all over to watch them. Like the Aurora Borealis, or Niagara Falls. I mean, they are huge and remarkable, aren't they? They would be quite a tourist attraction.' He grimaced.

'Seven years ago, about Michaelmas, or it may have been Lady Day, I fell asleep watching clouds like this. People argue with me, but I've always said it was seven years ago, and I always will. It was outside Cirencester, though I remember it being in Swaffham. You see the memory problem there perhaps. I lay on the sweet grass and fell asleep with my eyes open. That gave the white devils their opening. The clouds got in.'

'Into your eyes?'

'Into my brain. The damp clouds slid right into my mind. Asleep, I felt nothing but a little coldness, a slightly uncomfortable feeling of penetration. My memories were *nebulated.* That's what the doctor called it, or perhaps it was my mother or the Latin teacher. After that there were always patches of cloud in my memory – or mist, you could say. Because that's all they are really – damned bits of fog!' He shouted the word angrily and glanced upwards at his soft white enemies.

'The wet clouds slid through my brain, obscuring whatever they passed, now this, now that. They were extensive, and the effect was transformative and debilitating. I couldn't remember my wife or my job. Oh, in bits, in fragments. I remembered our holiday in Yarmouth, say, but not our wedding. I remembered the office, but not what I did there. My life fell apart completely, and I have never recovered.'

'Dreadful,' I said.

'Oh, you don't know. I mean the job; I miss the money but otherwise they know what they can do with it. But my wife? My wife, man? I loved her, but I lost her. She said I didn't remember who she was any more. And the worst of it is, she was right.' He let out a suppressed, frustrated moan. 'Those things up there, you think they're pillows or smiling piles of cotton wool. Marshmallows. But they are demons of the damp just as Satan is a demon of the fire, and they are malicious.'

'Well,' I said, 'I suppose the grey ones...'

'The grey ones? You think the *colour* makes any difference? They are agents of decay, man. They resent our solidity and wish they could dissolve it. Don't risk letting them in. I'm telling you.'

We sat in silence for a while, contemplating the evil nature of white fluffy clouds.

'So your mind has patches of cloud in it?' I asked.

'Oh no. Not now. They're all gone now. But it's worse than ever.'

'What happened?'

'It rained. In my brain. There was a gigantic storm, and they all turned to water and washed away. But the flood did terrific damage. It wrecked great swathes of my mind. My memories, my thoughts, were left in flitters and tatters.'

'I'm sorry,' I said.

'You don't know. You don't know what it was. You can't understand how badly my thoughts have been wrecked. You're probably thinking of my seventh birthday party where the best man made a speech about our marketing strategy. But that's nothing. Mild confusion. Most of it is much worse than that. What are the novels of George Eliot? A blow on the elbow, a snatch of music and three Cumberland sausages: that's my recollection. In my mind, the second day of the week is a yellow voice shouting in a corridor and my grandmother's face is a radio programme about Mannerist art. You have no idea how horrid that is. So don't look. Don't ever let those spongy white erasers into your head. Please.'

'Thank you for the warning,' I said.

After a few moments he grunted, stood up and set off down the path to the village. I watched him go, and when he had quite disappeared, I tipped my head back and stared at the clouds again. But it wasn't the same anymore and I knew it never would be.

Peter Hankins spent many years pecking out a novel on his iPad while sitting with his elbows pressed to his sides on London commuter trains. In those days he had a civil service job where his ability to write prose that sounded misleadingly authoritative was one of his chief assets. He had a long-running blog Conscious Entities about consciousness and now has a newer one Seen and Done (seen-and-done.com) about writing and other projects by him and others. Since retiring with chronic health problems in the shape of Crohn's disease, he has focused his energy on writing short stories, for fun and in order to build up his writing skills. His stories have been placed or shortlisted in a number of competitions.

ALSO BY OXFORD FLASH FICTION PRIZE

AN OXFORD FLASH FICTION PRIZE ANTHOLOGY
STICKS AND STONES
THE GREATS IN FLASH FICTION
EDITED BY FJ MORRIS

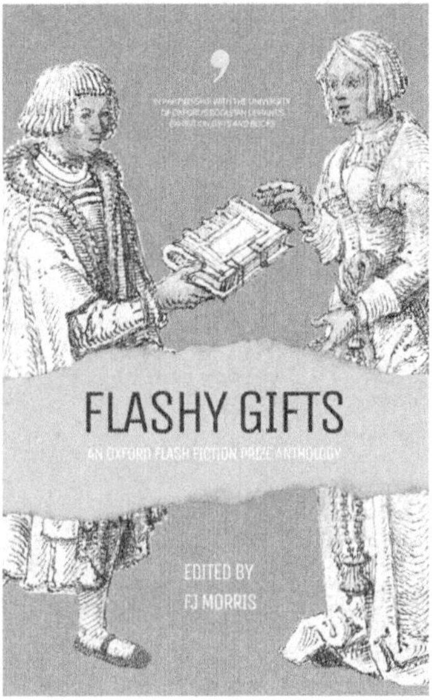
FLASHY GIFTS
AN OXFORD FLASH FICTION PRIZE ANTHOLOGY
EDITED BY
FJ MORRIS

BUT WORDS
CAN NEVER
HURT ME
THE GREATS IN FLASH FICTION
EDITED BY FJ MORRIS